MISCHIEF CORNER BOOKS PRESENTS

Uncommonly
Tidy
Poltergeists

ANGEL MARTINEZ

About the Book You Have Purchased:

This copy is intended for the original purchaser of this book ONLY. No part of this book may be reproduced, scanned, or distributed in any printed or electronic form without prior written permission from the authors. Please do not participate in or encourage piracy of copyrighted materials in violation of the author's rights. Purchase only authorized editions.

Cover Artist: LC Chase
Editor: Jude Dunn

First Edition

ISBN-13: **978-1540755872**
ISBN-10: **1540755878**

PUBLISHER
Mischief Corner Books, LLC

Dedication

For everyone who has ever been told that they are broken because they are different—you are no more a broken person than a Dali is a broken painting.

Angel Martin

Trademarks Acknowledgement

The author acknowledges the trademarked status and trademark owners of the following word marks mentioned in this work of fiction:

Aldi: Aldi Einkauf GmbH & Compagnie, oHG
Bon Ami: Bon Ami Company
The Exorcist: Warner Bros. Entertainment, Inc.
Jetway: John Bean Technologies Corporation
Kawasaki Versys: Kawasaki,
Klingon: CBS Studios, Inc.
Krug Grande Cuvée: LVMH Moët Hennessy Louis Vuitton SE
Poltergeist: MGM Holdings Inc.
Rebel: Honda Motor Co., Ltd.
REWE: The REWE Group
Styrofoam: The Dow Chemical Company
Valium: Roche Holding AG
Vlasic: Pinnacle Food Group, LLC

Table of Contents

Chapter One
Dinner in Kennett Square

Taro fidgeted in his chair, as nervous as when he'd confessed to skipping class in high school. A class, singular, but the crushing remorse afterward had expanded it in his mind into a criminal act. The unease was ridiculous now—he had *good* news to spill—but his stomach wouldn't settle. Everything still had a surreal quality to it tinged with creeping guilt, as if any moment someone would show up and say it was all a mistake or worse, that Taro had unwittingly committed some sort of fraud.

He waited for a lull in conversation, not an easy thing, since both Ben and Luka had brought their families for Sunday dinner. It had been a regular thing years ago for their parents to have the whole family over, but Ray had moved out west, and Ben and Luka had been moving progressively farther away with each addition to their respective families. Now, most weeks it was just Mom, Papi, and Taro, since he still lived in town. Alone. Again.

Once his nieces and nephews had been freed from the onerous chore of sitting at the table with the old people and their moms had followed to referee, Taro made an attempt. "I drove ... down to Dover a few weeks ago."

"To the farmer's market?" Ben said around a mouthful of pie. "Long way to go for strawberries."

Luka gave Ben an odd look. "He didn't say anything about produce."

"Well, no, but why else go all the way—" Ben tried to defend his conclusion-jumping, but Mom interrupted him.

"It was to go to some specialist down there, wasn't it?" Her tone was hard, but there was undisguised horror in her eyes. "Taro, are you sick? Why didn't you tell us?"

"Holy shit," Ben whispered. "That idiot Craig infected you? Should we even have the kids around you? Little germ carriers. That could be bad if your immune system isn't working right."

"That's not how it works." Luka's forehead creased in annoyance. "Don't start spreading misinform—"

"So you're a medical doctor now?"

"No, but I treat patients with HIV. I have to *inform* myself."

Taro folded his napkin into a precise triangle, then successively smaller ones while he waited for his brothers' pissing contest to die down. Nothing new, of course. Ben was the oldest and always knew best. Luka was the one with the psychology degrees and should've known better. Had Ray been there, he would've been just as likely to egg Ben on as to try to mediate.

"You *could* all stop making wild guesses and let Taro tell you," Papi said without taking his attention from his pie or raising his voice. "Just a suggestion."

The jumble of voices stilled as if he had bellowed, Ben still glaring and their mother's expression stating quite clearly that heads would roll if she didn't have answers quickly.

"I won the lottery," Taro blurted out.

"That's all?" Mom crushed her napkin in her fist. "This is a good thing. You couldn't tell us a *good* thing?"

"Lise, please," Papi soothed. "I think there's more."

Luka leaned back in his chair. "Yes. Like why you had to drive all the way to Dover."

Taro cleared his throat. Mom was right. This was a good thing, or it would be if he could rid himself of the nagging anxiety. "I don't usually play. But the Powerball was so huge, I thought, why not? I bought five tickets in Hockessin instead of here because Delaware has nondisclosure. Just in case. When the numbers matched on one, I was excited, but I was sure I'd be sharing the prize with other people."

"Well, fuck," Ben whispered.

"Language," Mom snapped automatically, but she was staring at Taro.

"I went to Dover to claim the prize. There were none ... no other winners."

Luka placed a hand on Taro's, ebony covering Taro's copper. It was probably to stop Taro's shaking, though Luka trembled as well. "Tar? How much are we talking here?"

Taro had signed papers and been advised by the lottery commission representatives. The figures had stared at him from the page, but he hadn't had to say it yet. If he said it, it would be real. Taro pulled in a fortifying breath. "Millions. Hundreds of millions. It's ... I ..."

"Overwhelming?" Luka offered.

"Yes."

Papi was the first to shake his paralysis, reaching over to fold Taro in a bear hug. "Congratulations. This is wonderful!"

"Thank you, Papi. I think ... it is? The whole thing makes me nervous." Taro looked around the table from face to face. "And please, please. You can't tell *anyone*."

"Not even Raymond?" Mom asked.

"I'll tell Ray. But I don't want it public. I don't want anyone but us to know. The horror stories about lottery winners being hounded? I just can't." Taro pulled in another breath, still holding onto Papi and Luka to keep him steady. "I want to set up funds for the kids. Funds for all of you that you can pull from. Mom, Papi, I'd like to buy you the place in Florida you've always wanted."

A general uproar ensued, during which his family objected strongly to his doling out his winnings. Some of his anxiety calmed in the face of their unwavering support, and he felt silly for worrying about their reactions. Taro held up a hand to ask for quiet. "There'll be plenty left. This is more money than I can spend in five lifetimes."

"Here's my question, then." Luka squeezed his hand once more before he let go. "What do you want to do? Not for anyone else, but for you."

Taro chewed on his bottom lip, the gnawing anxiety creeping back in. "I'm not sure yet. I think... It's that I'm afraid I won't do the right thing. That I'll be wasting it. Maybe I *should* just give it all away. I've known about this for three weeks, and I'm still going to work every day, pretending nothing's happened."

"One of the things you want to do is give back," Luka prompted gently.

"Yeah. But even that's overwhelming."

Papi tapped his fork on the table absently. "Taro, you make it sound like you have to solve everything at once."

"I don't—" Taro cut himself off, his face heating. That was exactly what he'd been trying to do. Resolve all his questions before he could move in any direction. Put all the funds in neat little boxes where they would be orderly and safe. "Okay. So maybe I was."

Ben let out a barking laugh, though he tried to

turn it into a cough, while Luka looked like he was struggling. Mom glared them into sheepish silence. Two grown fathers, and she still had that power.

"So you decide which things are most important to you, and you give money to those places now." Mom gave a little shrug. "You can always give to other things later."

"Then you can focus on what you want to do." Luka prodded at Taro's shoulder. "If you're happy working in accounting, that's great. Do that. But I think you might have decided on that degree for practical reasons. You used to love so many things."

"History," Ben offered.

"Geography," Papi said. "All those maps and books. Anthropology."

Taro held up both hands. "I know. I *have* been thinking about it. It's not that I hate accounting. Numbers are my friends. They always have been. But I do want ... something more. I *have* been thinking about something, and you'll all think I'm crazy. I want to travel."

Ben's right eyebrow shot up. "That's not crazy. You hardly ever even take days off."

"Right. That's not ..." Taro had the oddest feeling that he should shout, *But wait, there's more!* "I don't want to travel as a tourist. I want to be a traveler and write about travel, but I want to do it from the perspective of someone who lives in the places he's—*I'm* writing about."

"You're moving away?" Mom's frown couldn't have been any clearer regarding what she thought of that.

"Taro's never going to get this out if we don't let him talk." Luka held a finger up to his lips, the closest anyone would dare come to telling their mother to be quiet.

He'd spent his life safe and content under his older brothers' protective shadows, never insisting on being the center of attention, happy to watch and listen. His parents had refereed family meals for decades, first with foster kids in the early years of their marriage, then with three small boys when they adopted first Ray, then brothers Ben and Luka. Taro had been the late surprise addition, born long after his parents had given up on having biological children of their own. By that time, Luka, the youngest, had already been ten. It wasn't that Taro felt overshadowed. He *liked* listening. Absorbing. Being the center of his family's attention was unsettling.

Taro drummed his fingers on the table. "What I want to do is start buying houses ... property. Whatever kind makes sense in cities around the world. These would be my homes, but I'd have them all over. Stay a couple of weeks, get to know the area, then travel to the next house. I'd keep a running travelogue like Mark Twain did with his travels. Not as funny as Mark Twain, probably, but I could share my experiences and observations."

Papi's expression hovered between amusement and alarm. "You want to be a travel writer?"

"You'll always be out of the country?" Mom was about as far from amused as she could get. "We'll never see you. What about Christmas?"

"Yes, Papi. And no, Mom, I won't be. I do want some properties here in the US too. One in New York, at least. That won't be far."

Mom changed tactics. "You were so homesick spending a few weeks with your friend in Thailand."

"I was fifteen, Mom," Taro said with a soft laugh. "I'd never even been out of the state before, and Kathy was visiting family, so everyone knew each other except me."

"If you do this, you won't know *anyone*."

"Not at first, but this will be different. I'm not a teenager at the mercy of adult decisions. I'll be able to come and go on my own schedule. Do as much or as little as I'm comfortable with."

"Lise, *mi vida*." Papi had that twist to his mouth that meant he was trying hard not to smile. "Taro has a chance to do things he never would've thought of before. To have adventures. See the world. Don't make him feel guilty for having that chance."

"And I promise I'll be home for Christmas."

"See? He promises to be home for Christmas."

Mom's mouth was still set in a hard line, but she nodded. "All right. But he better not forget how to use a telephone."

* * * * *

"Mr. Torres?" A woman in a sharp gray business suit stepped out of the shadow of the building's *porte cochere*. Her heels put her well over six feet. The dark hair piled atop her head put her in giant territory.

"Yes. Hello." Taro offered his hand, and she shook it with fierce determination.

"I'm Andel Caruso, your property manager."

"I'm sorry, did you say Angel?"

"No." The scowl was brief and ferocious. "It's Andel, not Angel. Let's get you inside, and I'll show you around."

Taro wanted to apologize, but Andel had obviously moved on, already striding inside. He scurried on his legs of inferior size to keep up. Everything inside the lobby gleamed: the tiled floor, the walls, and the art deco inspired elevators. He'd seen it on the whirlwind tour with the real estate agent, of course, but all the shiny hadn't registered.

Andel waved a hand in Taro's general direction as they passed the security desk. "This is Mr. Torres. Just bought seventeen-oh-two."

The guard only glanced at him and nodded

without demands to see ID or proof of ownership. Taro had to get over the creeping guilt of being somewhere he felt he didn't belong. He *had* been at the settlement. That had been him signing all those documents. A lovely Manhattan condominium, Central Park West, was legally his.

Andel leaned against the back of the elevator cracking her gum. Taro found himself staring.

"Do I have broccoli in my teeth?"

"Ah, no. It's ... the gum. Caught me off guard." *Since the rest of you is spit-and-polish business.*

"Sorry about that. Trying to quit the cancer sticks for good."

"How's it going?"

"Craving's kicking my ass like you wouldn't believe. Is it bothering you?"

"Not at all. Whatever you need to do to stop."

She nodded, regarding him with narrowed eyes. "You seem like a nice man, Mr. Torres. Is there a Mrs. Torres? Another Mr. Torres? Kids?"

Taro shook his head. "No. It's just me." *It is, isn't it? It's really just me.* He'd always had family right there to catch him between boyfriends. Then there'd been Craig hanging over his head for ... had it really been that long? Somehow, his relationship with Craig had managed to limp and stagger along for five years. This sudden flying solo hadn't made him lonely, exactly, but it was a little disorienting if he thought about it too hard.

"Just wanted the extra space? Three bedrooms?"

"In case family visits. Maybe for the holidays."

Andel took off at top speed again when the elevator doors opened. "You just shoot me a message whenever you'll be in town, Mr. Torres. I'll have the cleaning crew come through and set up a grocery delivery."

"Is that ... usual?"

She gave him an odd sideways look as she opened the door. "It's my job, Mr. Torres. Don't your other property managers?"

Taro walked over to the living room windows. The floor-to-ceiling view out over the park cause a touch of unexpected vertigo, so he stepped back. He'd had a nice apartment in Kennett Square all those years, comfortable, but he suspected most of it could have fit in this room.

"I don't own any other properties yet. That's something I'm working on. I'd like... This is either going to sound silly or incredibly arrogant. I'd like to have them circumnavigating the globe."

When he turned to Andel though, her expression was far from judgmental. Calculating would've been a better word. "So you've never bought property outside the country? Do you have an attorney? Someone who does international real estate law?"

"Not yet."

She nodded. "I don't want to sound pushy or anything, but I know this guy..."

This guy turned out to be an efficient and expensive expert in international property law. The fees were shocking, and Taro had to calm the minor storm in his stomach before he could remind himself that he could afford them. Better to have a good attorney than to deal with a legal mess later.

Taro spent the next six months in New York purchasing a few things for the condo, exploring the city, getting his passport renewed, and signing enough papers that he could've built another house from them. Travel plans he handled himself. Any bit of direct control he could retain over his life rather than relying on other people was a relief.

Finally, he was ready. Twelve properties waited for him around the globe, and he'd allowed himself a week at each in his itinerary. Three months to see if he could sustain and enjoy his experiment. He could always make adjustments later, but the excitement, the *fever* of travel had him in its teeth.

Taro, who had rarely left his hometown and had been out of the country a grand total of once, was off to see the world.

Chapter Two
Glasses in Marburg

Eight clean glasses. Taro took them out of the cabinet in the dining room and held each one up to the light. Clean. All of them.

"I know I didn't ..." he trailed off as he hurried back to the kitchen. Bad habit, talking to himself.

He'd come in after midnight on a delayed flight too tired to think about unpacking, drank a glass of water, left the glass on the counter—water ring and all—and went to bed. Now, the glass had been cleaned and put away and the counter wiped down. Taro checked the doors and windows in case he'd had a neat-freak burglar break in, but the house was locked tight.

"Sleepwalking. Everything's been so weird, I've started sleepwalking."

Already he was rethinking touring his new properties a week at a time. He needed to extend his stay in each place. As soon as he felt settled, his self-imposed schedule moved him on to the next house or condo or villa. A week had seemed so long when he'd made the plans in New York. With travel, time changes, and adjusting to a new place every Sunday, it was all much more grueling than he could have imagined.

Breakfast. Marburg. I am in Marburg, right?

He checked his itinerary, went outside to look at the front of the house, and confirmed that, yes, he was indeed in his newly-purchased country house outside Marburg. Of his twelve properties, this wasn't the biggest or the most unique, but the little *fachwerk* house had a quiet charm, tucked away behind ancient trees and nestled beside a softly chattering stream.

"This is a good place to get my head back together," he told the robin singing in the bush by the door. Talking to a bird was not talking to yourself, right? He was guessing about the robin part too. Tiny guy with a red front, nothing like the big, attitudinal robins back home.

Frau Voss, the housekeeper, had left eggs and bread for him, and coffee beans, bless her. With a soft-boiled egg—boiled six minutes and twenty seconds precisely—a heavenly cup of dark coffee, a thick slice of fresh bread with honey, and his laptop, Taro settled on the patio in the back garden to regroup and plan.

His notes on Marburg had him scheduled to visit the castle and the old gardens that day, the next items in a long list of sightseeing since he'd left his home base in New York. He'd managed to keep to his schedule up until that morning. *I'm just too damn tired today. My feet hurt, my back hurts, my everything hurts.*

Maybe if he'd been twenty-five instead of nearing forty, he might have kept up the grueling schedule. From New York to Chicago to San Francisco, a week in each city had been fine. He'd been running on adrenaline and excitement. The first exhaustion crash had hit him in Hawaii after several airline delays and the long flight, but his house on the big island set back in the ohia trees had been the perfect place to recuperate. Slower pace, perfect weather, and he'd been ready to go again.

Then came Tokyo, Chiang Mai, Chandigarh, Paris and Barcelona, all with too much he wanted to see, too much to take in at once. Near the end of his first world tour, Taro knew he wasn't doing so well. Sleep-washing of glassware was proof of that.

"No tourist stuff today," he told the robin who had joined him in the backyard to partake of the ornate ceramic birdbath. "I'm going through my notes and napping. That's the plan."

His spot on the slate patio was comfortably warm. The neighborhood was blissfully quiet. Taro woke with a start when footsteps crunched on the gravel path at the side of the house. His coffee was cold, but at least he'd finished his egg.

"Yoo-hoo! *Herr* Torres, are you here?" A sturdy woman in sensible slacks and a button-down shirt strode around the corner, waving when she spotted him. "*Guten morgen*! I'm Helga Voss, your housekeeper. I was ringing at your doorbell, but you did not answer."

Taro struggled up from his patio chair and held out a hand. "Frau Voss, I'm so sorry. Must've fallen asleep. Very nice to meet you."

She nodded and shook his hand in a no-nonsense way. "You have been doing much traveling, I've heard. Maybe too much. I am here to see if everything is in order for you and to ask if you have a shopping list for me."

"Shopping list?"

"Yes. I left a few things for you, but I did not know what you like yet. Maybe I should have asked by email." She shrugged. "I did not think of it."

"I ... Oh." Taro struggled for words. People wanting to *do* things for him still made him uncomfortable. He had changed what he did for a living but not so much how he lived. "I think ... Would it be all right if I come shopping with you? I'd like to get to know the area. Do the shopping myself when I'm here?"

Frau Voss stared at him. "So. You pay me to clean an empty house that does not need cleaning and look after a little garden that does not want much. You come for a week at a time and do not intend to let me do what I should. I feel as if I am stealing your money, Herr Torres."

"No, no!" Taro waved one hand over the other. He supposed what she said made sense. A house that stayed shut up with no one living in it wouldn't need much cleaning. "I don't ... I'm just used to doing things myself. I think ... What I think I need is an ear and a guide right now. Someone to listen and help me plan and orient myself. Could we do that? Have some coffee with me and help me feel like a person again and not a butterfly?"

The frown didn't ease, but she nodded, strode past him into the house, and soon returned with a heated carafe and a second cup. "So. Tell me what it is you do, Herr Torres."

"Taro. Please." The tight guilt in his stomach eased as he settled back in his chair. "I suppose I don't really do anything right now."

"It is family money, then?"

Taro blinked at the sharp tone. Of course. Most likely, he was either the lazy spawn of a wealthy tycoon or a criminal in her mind right now. "No. My family never had much, and I've had decent jobs, but nothing special. Accounting sorts of things. One day I bought lottery tickets. I don't usually, but the jackpot was so huge."

He told her all if it—the disbelief, the anxiety, the strange despair that he wouldn't do the right things; the final separation of funds into annuities for taxes and living expenses and for family members; trust funds for youth centers, scholarships, and medical research; the house in Florida for his parents, and finally, the global ring of real estate for his travels.

"It has been very confusing for you." Frau

Voss sipped her coffee, still frowning. Her expression hadn't so much as twitched during his recitation. "Travel is important. But what is it that you do, Herr Torres? You cannot simply wander aimlessly from place to place."

Taro ducked his head. "You'll probably think it's silly."

"I may. Though I do not know unless you say."

With a wave at the laptop containing all his photos and notes, he said, "I want to be a travel writer. Like Rick Steves or someone. I want to show people what's out there besides taking selfies at tourist spots. Understand other places so I can share them. I'd ... only left the country once before. Rarely left my home."

She nodded, her frown suddenly less fierce. "Why Marburg? Why not Berlin or Frankfurt or Munich?"

"My mother was born here. I wanted to get to know the city where she grew up." He pointed with his chin at the house. "And now I have a place here where she can visit with me."

Frau Voss put her coffee cup down in a crisp, decisive manner. "Where did your mother live?"

"I don't... I guess I don't know."

"You have a phone, I'm sure. Call her. I will take you shopping and then take you there."

Taro jumped up to find his phone, her sharp tone and a new, strange thought driving him. Nine properties and seven countries into his journey, he'd finally had a real conversation with someone. Maybe the lack of real interaction was contributing to the strained disorientation of his extended journey.

Grocery stores weren't something Taro had researched in his itineraries, so the number of them around the city surprised him. Just because he lived in a cute country house and narrow winding streets of medieval houses occupied much of the center of the city, he hadn't been expecting modern grocery stores. Little corner stores for milk and eggs, yes. Bakeries and *Konditoreien*, those lovely confectioner shops where you could stop in for a slice of cake and coffee, yes. The Aldi and the REWE out by the Erlenring? Not so much.

Discovery about a city was *good*, of course—that was the whole point to his travels—but he was embarrassed about his assumptions.

For her part, Frau Voss was more interested in grilling him on his food and condiment preferences, insisting on building a standing list with which she could stock the house prior to his visits.

Groceries procured, Frau Voss had parked the car and walked with him to Weidenhäuser Strasse, one of the charming cobblestone streets where the old houses leaned in on either side as if they were eavesdropping on passing conversations. As long as they weren't physically dropping eaves, Taro thought he could live with that.

She stopped in front of a three-story house with a sharply sloping roof, its bright white walls crisscrossed with brown *fachwerk* beams. "This one."

"This one? It's so..."

"Yes?"

"Cute. Storybook cute. Wow."

"Your mother had no pictures of her parents' house?"

Taro checked behind him and took a few steps back to make certain there would be pictures now. "She had photographs from when she was little. But all the pictures were people. There weren't any of the house. It's *so* cute. The sun carvings on the door, oh my god."

When he glanced at Frau Voss, she had that tight-lipped smile of the rigidly reserved, but her eyes had crinkled at the corners—probably the closest she was willing to come to laughing at him. "It is a wonderful house, *Herr* Torres."

His big goofy grin persisted, and he felt lighter than he had since he'd started this journey. He'd been so focused on sites that he'd forgotten *this* was what he'd set out to do, to share a connection to places rather than just a checklist of things to see. Of course, this was his first time around the globe, and he *was* a tourist still. He was determined to get better at this with more experience, though he had to admit not being alone had helped a great deal.

Maybe a traveling companion? He realized with a dull ache that Craig would've made the whole experience much more difficult. Complaints about beds, food, service, traffic, unfamiliar smells, Taro getting lost—Craig had been a pain just going to the Poconos. Taro had excused it because of Craig's headaches, which had probably been as fictitious as every other Craig excuse.

Wanted: fellow traveler. Must be open-minded and considerate. Self-centered liars need not apply.

Someday, perhaps, but Taro was done putting his life on hold for someone else. He'd come to that conclusion even before the lottery win.

At the end of the day, as Frau Voss helped him put his groceries away, Taro was wilting with exhaustion. So much for not moving from the house that day. After he thanked his housekeeper/tour guide and said goodnight, he made himself a teewurst sandwich, dragged himself upstairs, and ate his dinner in bed. The plate would just have to sit on the bedside table until morning. He wasn't moving again unless the house caught fire.

* * * * *

The next morning he woke to the sun streaming through lace curtains, his robin friend singing in the hazelnut bush outside, and no plate on the table. Taro wandered downstairs, yawning, to find the plate and the knife he'd used the night before washed and put away. At least he felt better rested, but he hoped the sleep-cleaning thing wasn't going to become a habit.

Chapter Three
Ashes in Wales

Taro's draconic itinerary dragged him from his Marburg house too soon, and the next Sunday found him riding in a hired car to his property in Wales.

The hobbit house near Hay-on-Wye was ridiculously charming, built entirely of scrap wood and dug out of a hillside. Care, practicality, and artistry suffused the careful construction, from the beautifully fitted round door painted Kelly green, to the solar panels that provided hot water and electricity.

Officially, the realty listing could only describe five rooms—the front parlor, the kitchen, the bedroom and attached bath, and a little study tucked in the back against the hill—but the house boasted so many ledges and nooks, crannies and extra cubbyholes it felt much larger than the official square footage implied.

Taro unlocked the door and sneezed. *Okay, so this house doesn't have a Helga Voss taking care of it.* Might have been good to know ahead of time, but the property manager here wasn't great about answering messages. Taro didn't mind some housework. His plan was to concentrate on how living here would work, not sightseeing. Cleaning up would help him get to know the house.

Eventually, he would explore Hay-on-Wye and the surrounding countryside properly, but not this week. He'd brought some freeze-dried food and tea in his luggage, so even shopping could wait a day or two. After he stashed his suitcases in the bedroom with its platform alcove for the bed and the adorable round window, he searched through cabinets and closets for cleaning supplies.

All he found was an ancient, nearly empty can of Bon Ami under the sink. No sponges, no cleaning rags, no scrub brushes and no hint of a vacuum lurked anywhere on the premises. A quick peek through the front windows showed heavy clouds and rain beginning to speckle the path, so pedaling the beat-up old bicycle that came with the house into town wasn't a good idea. Annoyed and fighting a quickly deteriorating mood, Taro decided on a nice fire in the wood stove and some tea, dust be damned.

"All right, stove, let's see if you're useable."

Taro crouched in front of the cast-iron monstrosity in the front parlor and averted his face while he eased the door open. No cascade of ash and dust greeted him, at least. Inside the stove was relatively clean. Dry wood and kindling sat neatly in the bin beside it. Good. Several good things to offset the bad, and at least building a good fire was in Taro's short list of skills.

Using some crackly old newspapers he'd

found in a closet and an old-fashioned striker, he hummed contentedly when the kindling caught. He was waiting for the teakettle to boil in the kitchen when things began to go wrong again. The light from the kitchen window suddenly had a hazy quality. He expected the scent of a wood fire, but this was too strong. Alarmed, he rushed back to the front room to find a film of blue smoke hanging in the air. Some of the wood must have been wet.

When he opened the door on the wood stove, black smoke billowed out, too thick to see if the fire had gone out.

"Damn it." Taro slammed the door shut and listened to the rain pouring down outside. A nest or weeds probably blocked the chimney, and he needed to go out to clear it.

Since he hadn't packed boots or a waterproof jacket, he stomped out in his sneakers and hoodie, up the hill and onto the grass-covered roof of the house. In the downpour, he was soaked to the skin before he found the chimney poking up through the meadow grass. A conical cap topped it, but no nests or brush obstructed the opening. Taro knelt, the knees of his jeans immediately soaked through on the wet ground, and angled his flashlight beam down the stack. Nothing.

He couldn't just go back into a smoke-filled house ... *Oh, crap.*

Stomach tight and aching with frustration, he

charged back into the house, banged his foot on the wall as he rushed to toe off his shoes, and hurried to the wood stove. Just as he'd feared, the little flat knob on the side of the chimney was parallel to the floor. He gave it a quarter turn, hoping it would help still.

"Always open the flue before you start a fire. Dummy." He kept muttering angry things at himself as he stomped around to shut the front door, turn on the exhaust vents in the kitchen and the bathroom, and peel out of his rain-heavy clothes. Too discouraged for either tea or another try at a cozy fire, he crawled naked into bed under the down comforter and tried to stop shivering.

This was why he never tried new things. *This* was the real reason he rarely left home. He was an incompetent disaster at too many practical things not job-related. Money hadn't changed any of that.

Eventually, he drifted off into uneasy dreams with mice in strange tunnels and a man trying to sell him smokeless cigars.

Sunbeams caressed the bed when he woke the next morning. Somehow waking up warm and dry with birds singing just outside the window made things manageable. He could do this, get the place cleaned up and livable. Dressing in what he hoped were well-considered layers—T-shirt, button-down, cardigan, dry jeans, and socks—he thought he would open the windows and the front door to air out the place while he heated some soup for breakfast.

He opened the bedroom door humming *Morning Has Broken* and stopped short.

"What in ...?"

The front room still had a smoky odor, but the fans had cleared the haze from the air. That wasn't shocking. No. Taro stood blinking at gleaming wood surfaces and a clean-swept floor. His hoodie hung from a peg by the door. His sneakers were mud free and lined up neatly by the round front door. He wandered to the kitchen to find his unused tea mug put away and the kettle emptied. Even worse, when he started to poke around, he couldn't find evidence of a single thing that could have been used to clean the dust off every surface in the house. This made less than zero sense. Negative sense.

His text query to the property manager about sending cleaning staff over that morning received a speedy and terse response.

No one sent to that address.

The doors and windows remained locked. Taro even checked the closets in case a serial cleaner had hidden in one. Only one possibility remained.

"Something's very wrong with me," he whispered as he sank down in the rocking chair by the wood stove. "Very, very wrong."

No matter how much he wanted to, he couldn't

call his parents. They would worry too much. His "friends" back home had all been work friends, and he had disappeared as quietly and anonymously as possible with horror stories about lottery winners who had gone public firmly in mind.

Instead, he sent a message to Luka. It might have been the longest text message he ever sent, and it would probably freak his brother out when he woke up, but not as badly as their nearly octogenarian mom and dad.

He stared at his phone while nibbling on a granola bar. Maybe part of it was missed meals and bad nutrition. Not that he'd eaten badly in Marburg. Frau Voss had made sure of that. The thought made him shiver. He'd never needed a minder before. Independent. Adult. Responsible.

The reply came back within ten minutes: *Taro? Do you need me to come out there?*

Tempting, but he couldn't ask Luka to do that. *No. I'll be all right. I think I'm just tired. But have you ever heard of anything like this?*

Are you on anything?

Taro snorted. *You know I don't use.*

I mean a sleep aid. Some people have reactions where they sleep drive and do other things they don't recall.

Oh. No. Nothing like that.

OK. You've been stressed, Tar. About lots of stuff. It was bound to catch up.

But do I need help? Should I find a hospital?

I can't answer that for you. If you feel you need to go in, go. But here's what I suggest.

Taro waited, leg bouncing in agitation.

Luka finally sent: *Clean up before you go to bed. Take care of anything that might be nagging at you. You've always been neat. I can see leaving dishes out or having layers of dust on things eating at your subconscious while you sleep. Then close and lock your bedroom door. Booby-trap it so you'll make a loud noise if you open it. That way you'll know if you've gotten up to clean while you were sleeping.*

That made sense. *But how do I stop doing it?*

Another long pause while Luka typed. *I think it sounds like sleepwalking. When you start to relax and feel less stressed again, it should stop. But Tar—if it doesn't, you make an appointment with your doctor, OK?*

I know, Luk. Don't nag.

They'll probably want to do sleep studies and stuff. Sure you don't want me to come out? Where the hell are you, anyway?

Wales. Very pretty here. No. I'll be fine. One more stop, then home to NY.

OK. If you're sure. Love you. Stay safe.

Thanks, Luk. Love you too.

Luka signed off with heart emojis and Taro smiled. Just remembering that someone out there worried about him helped. He could manage this weird sleep-cleaning. It would be all right.

Deep breath. Tea. Granola. Taro opened the door and breathed in the fresh scent of damp earth and grass, the wisteria blooming by the door. *I'll be fine. Everything's fine.*

Hay-on-Wye turned out to be as charming as the hobbit house, a town of lovely eateries, cozy shops, and books. All the books. Taro wondered if they had more bookstores per person than any other town. There were obvious tourists with the phones extended to snap pictures, but the town certainly wasn't overrun with them.

He stopped at a little grocery to pick up a few essentials, and the woman behind the counter eyed him strangely when he set his milk, eggs, bread, and cheese down.

"Staying hereabouts, sir?"

"Yes, ma'am. Just here for the week this time around, but I'll be back. Bought a little hobbit house outside of town."

"The Davies place?"

He nodded, suddenly anxious about where this was going.

"You do know that old mister Davies died there not two months ago." Again she was eyeing him sidelong.

"Oh? No, I didn't." Taro swallowed hard. "Was he a nice man?"

The shopkeeper shrugged. "He was a bit skinny. But not a bad sort."

Taro had the feeling he was missing something in translation. "I guess if he's not quite moved on, we'll get along all right."

He said it with a smile, but the shopkeeper shook her head and muttered something about Americans before she turned away. As he left the shop, he cringed. Yeah, that probably had sounded a little odd and creepy. Embarrassed and tired, he secured his groceries in his backpack and pedaled back the way he'd come. Hay-on-Wye desperately called for some more careful poking around, but he no longer felt up to it.

The embarrassment only kicked up several notches when he was cycling out of town. He turned his head longingly to gaze at yet another bookshop, and was sideswiped by a rude lamppost. He waved off a few concerned passersby with reassurances and a laugh. At least he'd only toppled sideways, so the groceries were safe.

Tomorrow. He would try again tomorrow.

A toasted cheese and a cozy fire sans smoke later, Taro settled in the big rocker by the wood stove to read. Warm, dry, and fed, the comfortable, snug feeling seeped into his bones until he'd rocked himself off to sleep.

When he woke, shadows stalked the room, and he wasn't snug or comfortable any longer.

Old mister Davies died there not two months ago...

Embers still crackled and smoldered in the stove's belly. The chimney stack creaked as it cooled. Taro sat up slowly and set his blanket aside, heart jumping at every stray night sound. It was stupid to be afraid, like a kid dashing down the dark hall from the bathroom in the middle of the night. It was ridiculous.

Still he sat paralyzed, afraid to get up, afraid to turn his head. *Way to freak yourself out. Didn't even have to watch* The Ring *or anything.*

Claws scrabbled on the outside of the front window, shocking a cry from Taro as he bolted up and raced for the bedroom. He slammed the door and locked it, arranged the pots and pans in front of the threshold for the "alarm" he'd discussed with Luka, jumped into bed without undressing, and pulled the covers tight over his head.

Stupid, stupid, as if he were eight again and scared of the dark. He shivered in his blanket cave, reassuring himself the scratching had probably been a night bird or a bat trying to catch a moth at the window. The thought didn't immediately make him feel better. Sometime after midnight, he drifted into strange dreams of trying to serve tea to heavy-footed ants who kept bringing in tiny boxes.

When he woke, blessed sunlight kissed the room, banishing the dark's oppressive grip. Taro sat up and drew a long breath, easing the tight barrel hoops of tension around his ribcage. Silly.

That's what the previous night had been. *Grown person frightened of normal night sounds. Ridiculous.*

His cookware alarm system gleamed at the threshold, undisturbed. At least his stressed-out state hadn't resulted in him getting up to sleep-clean. He stacked the pots and pans to one side of the round door, unlocked it, and sauntered down the hallway to the front room, whistling. Today, he would pack a lunch and go for a bike ride, just take in the countryside and soak up some sun. No itinerary, no plans—the perfect day.

The shiny brand-new day came crashing down around him when he reached the rocking chair.

His blanket, now neatly folded when he had left it in a heap on the floor, lay draped across the arm of the rocking chair. His tea mug no longer stood on the side table beside the chair. Stomach tight with impending shivers, Taro hurried to the kitchen and opened the cabinet that held the dishes. The mug had been washed, dried and put away.

"No," Taro whispered as he shut the cabinet with shaking hands. "No, no, no. I had the door rigged. The pots were stacked too high to step over. I couldn't have—"

The thought struck so hard he had to cling to the counter. *I couldn't have.* The fear from the previous evening roared back like a storm surge in a sea cave. He wasn't alone here. Something had done this. Not someone, since by now he would have noticed a person hiding in this tiny house. Something was here with him.

"Mr. Davies?" he called out, his voice only squeaking on the last syllable. "I don't... Please don't feel like you have to clean up after me."

Although... Did that make sense? Didn't it? Mr. Davies couldn't have been in Marburg, right? Ghosts attached to places. At least that's what he'd heard. So if Mr. Davies was here, what had happened in Germany? And if there was no ghost, what was happening to him? Was something *following* him?

While daylight made everything less blindingly terrifying, it was still damn unsettling. Both prospects—the possibly supernatural and the one that pointed to Taro. He couldn't even begin to figure out how to deal ghosts, on the one hand. On the other, little bit of sleepwalking he could rationalize, but cleaning an entire neglected house in the night and disposing of the evidence without disturbing the barricade of cookware across his bedroom door? That sounded like more than sleepwalking.

He couldn't stay. Not like this. *One more house. I'll try one more.* The Prince Edward Island house was the last one before home, anyway. He was already interrupting his carefully planned scheduled, but visiting PEI would mean he'd met his goal and visited all the new properties. He could salvage that much.

With the key to the little hobbit house clutched tight in his fist, he waited outside for the taxi. Packing had been easy, since he hadn't taken the time to unpack entirely—or it would have been easy if his hands hadn't been trembling and clumsy. All the way to the airport, he berated himself for being a gutless coward. The entire time he waited in line for a ticket agent, his stomach churned with shame. Did the priest in *The Exorcist* run screaming? No. Did the father in *Poltergeist* flee from the house and abandon his family? No. Fine, maybe that one was a little extreme. He didn't have a cute six-year-old to rescue, and so far, whatever had been happening hadn't manifested as malevolent forces of evil.

He'd just had a few belongings moved around and gotten scared by the possibility of an elderly ghost. Or his brain malfunctioning. He tried to call Luka while he walked to the gate, but it went right to voicemail, which probably meant he was seeing a client. Again Taro thought about calling his mother, and again he discarded the notion. She would *hear* that he was upset and badger him until he told her, which would cause her to jump to some extreme conclusion. Maybe that wasn't unreasonable in this case, but he still didn't want his parents to worry.

He called Ben instead.

"You're not used to being alone," Ben said

after Taro had given him a short version of events minus the possibility of ghosts.

He'd found a relatively isolated seat at the gate, a strange quiet corner in a sea of noise. "That doesn't make sense. I've lived alone since a little after college."

"I know, Tar. But this is different. You lived alone but every day you'd go to work. See people you knew. Go visit Mom and Dad on the weekends. Stop in for dinner at our place when we still lived in town. Just about every day, you talked to someone you knew. You've been *alone* the past few weeks. Really isolated, from what it sounds like. Have you even called Mom?"

"Of course..." Had he? "Um, I called her from Hawaii."

"Uh-huh. Weeks ago. You've really stressed your brain out. Tried to do too much. With nobody to talk to."

Taro laughed, the sound nervous and tinny in his own ears. "I thought Luka had the psych degree."

"Doesn't mean he got all the brains, even if he thinks he did. Stop the globe-hopping and get your rich ass home."

For a moment, he considered. The thought had an iron-bitter taste to it though, giving up and scurrying home to the shelter of his family. He'd done it once after college. Never again. He was *not* falling apart, and he was going to figure things out like an independent adult. "I'm headed to Prince Edward Island now. Last stop before I'm back in New York. Drive up and see me when I get there?"

"Maybe when school's out. The kids have the Math Olympics coming up and softball..."

"It's fine, Ben. I get it." Taro conjured a smile so his big brother wouldn't hear the disappointment. "I'll see you soon."

He watched the luggage trucks zipping back and forth after he hung up, left foot bouncing at a steady jog until a man farther down the row glared at him. Maybe he *was* just lonely and should have someone with him for these trips. That couldn't explain what was happening though. Could it?

Chapter Four
Dust Herds on PEI

Driving on Prince Edward Island turned out to be surprisingly soothing. Taro had rented a car at the airport in Charlottetown for the drive to the eastern side of the island. Outside of the city, the roads were two-lane and lightly traveled, lined with evergreens and farm fields. He passed fewer and fewer vehicles as he drove through the afternoon.

The old two-story farmhouse on the northeast corner of the island was perfect, just as it had appeared in the real estate photos. It gleamed, white and inviting on the lonely road, its nearest neighbor an unassuming white church huddled beside a well-kept graveyard. A caretaker was mowing the grass between the headstones when Taro pulled up.

Perfect, peaceful, *bucolic*, with the sea a short walk down the road. The pastor who watched the property and provided him the key warned him that the place might be a bit rough. The house had been empty for two years. When Taro opened the side door that led into the kitchen, herds of dust bunnies and dust raccoons and dust sheep greeted him, but structurally it was sound. The windows were tight. The floors barely creaked. He shook his head at the general state of neglect and told himself he would clean up in the morning.

The kitchen was compact but still had room for a table and chairs. The refrigerator was an ancient model, the kind with a latch handle that they'd stopped making for safety reasons, but it ran just fine when Taro plugged it in. The rest of the downstairs was taken up by the dining room, with a table large enough to seat a family of ten, a den where creaky leather furniture lurked, and the front room where a battered old couch held court amidst dust-crowned bookshelves. A quick glance through titles hinted at a collection of books about local history and stories, which would be a wonderful find.

Though why the previous owner left them— strange.

Upstairs wasn't much better. The bedrooms situated along the long hallway of the second floor were just as dusty as downstairs, but at least the linens were in a tightly sealed closet. The sheets and towels had escaped the dusty fate of the rest of the house. Taro did find cleaning supplies (Hallelujah!) in the larger of the two bathrooms with a half-full container of furniture polish. He cleaned off the bed, nightstand, and bureau in the bedroom farthest from the stairs, since that one didn't have dust-laden curtains on the windows, and called it done for the night.

Once he'd made the bed, he was tired enough that he was sure he wouldn't move in his sleep, much less sleepwalk.

Just in case, he still raided the kitchen for pots and pans to set across his bedroom doorway as an alarm. While he was rummaging through the cabinets, he thought about sleepwalking versus ghosts. *You're supposed to make salt barriers for ghosts, aren't you?* Taro stood with the container of Morton's in one hand, feeling silly while the clock ticked off ten minutes. Finally, he shook out salt lines across the back-door threshold, the kitchen, the dining room, and the bedroom as well, just outside his cookware barrier. He hated to go to bed in a filthy house. The thought made his skin crawl, but he could barely keep his eyes open.

Stumbling with exhaustion, he locked the bedroom door and crawled under the covers, expecting that all his preparations would be intact when the sun rose and he would feel ridiculous.

The next morning, he had hope. His door remained locked. Nothing in his chosen bedroom appeared to have been disturbed, down to his carefully stacked wall of pots. Hope did a nose dive into the hardwood and died when he opened the door. The salt line across his doorway had vanished. The hallway floor gleamed. His heart decided a heavy *thud-thump* would be the best rhythm as he crept down the hall. The bathroom tiles sparkled. All the dust animals had been herded out of the bedrooms. Downstairs echoed the upstairs, every surface cleaned and polished, his salt lines all swept away. He stood in the middle of the kitchen trying to find a calm spot inside him and failing miserably.

"Okay, I can't do this," he said to the ancient refrigerator. It answered by kicking its compressor on with a sympathetic hum. "Whatever's happening here, I just can't. Not alone. If this is me, I'm scaring the hell out of me. And if it's not me, it's scaring the hell out of me more."

The fridge clicked and thumped before it went back to humming. Taro chose to interpret that as agreement.

"I need to get back home to regroup."

New York would be safe. He knew his place there was fine. Nothing out of the ordinary had ever happened in his six months there except for the pizza guy making a pass at him. It was home now, and he desperately needed to get back to people he knew, people whose advice he trusted. Maybe it was admitting defeat, but he was too anxiety-ridden and worn down to care anymore.

The house had no internet connection and a flickering bar of cell phone service, so Taro found himself using a telephone book and a landline phone from the fifties to call the airport for flight information. There was a flight to LaGuardia with only one stop in Halifax, but not until late that evening. It would have to do.

He cleaned up and packed, puttered through the library in the front room, and decided to drive to the little grocery down the road to pick up something for lunch. A whole loaf of bread would have been a waste, since he couldn't easily put it in his luggage. He bought a yogurt and an apple, which caused raised eyebrows on the elderly couple behind the counter.

"You on a diet, son?"

"Ha, um, no? I just have a flight to catch later." He blurted it out, startled by the question. That didn't seem to fly as an explanation, so he stumbled on. "I, ah, bought the Gillies' farmhouse up the road, but I can't stay long this trip. Has it been a while since anyone lived there?"

"Lived?" The old woman took his money in one gnarled hand and opened the cash drawer with the other. "No one's *lived* there since Martha Gillies died in, oh, I suppose it was nineteen-eighty or so."

"So it's been empty all this time?" *That would explain the condition of the house.*

"Well, no, not empty." The old man rummaged under the counter and found a plastic spoon for him. "Martha's boy, George, had the place. 'Course he was a professor of something or other in the states. Only came up in the summers. Was two years back, I think, he died up there on a visit."

Taro thanked them, gathered up his lunch, and drove back to the house. The house had two potential ghosts in it, which raised another frightening possibility. Did he *attract* ghosts? Did his presence wake them or rouse them or whatever one did with ghosts? If he did, why *cleaning* ghosts? The whole thing gave him a headache, and he still needed to make the drive to Charlottetown. He twitched as he locked up the house, turned off the empty fridge, and gathered his things to leave. A constant itching pressure between his shoulder blades convinced him something watched him. He wanted to *run* out of the house, but he had the bad feeling that running attracted attention. From whatever it was.

These peaks and valleys of fear had to be bad for him. His chest ached. His stomach was in knots. His head throbbed constantly with a low-grade ache that turned up a notch when his anxious thoughts escalated. Taro leaned his head against the steering wheel, forcing himself to breathe slowly. Home. Everything would feel better once he got home.

He didn't realize quite how tense every inch of him was until he nearly sobbed during touchdown at LaGuardia. The tiny grandmother sitting next to him reached over to pat his knee.

"Flying can be hard on a person," she murmured.

Unable to get any words out past his clenched

jaw, Taro nodded and concentrated on relaxing one abused muscle at a time. *Flying* wasn't the problem, but he couldn't just blurt out what was behind his fear. *No, ma'am, I'm being followed. Possibly by a ghost. Or several. Either that or I've been having psychotic breaks.*

He didn't care at all how bad he looked when he trudged to his door. Even when a woman walking toward him sidled away to the other side of the hall, he was too exhausted to apologize for looking like patient zero for the zombie apocalypse. Jittery from caffeine so he wouldn't fall asleep in the cab, he couldn't rest yet. So he sorted his laundry, checked to see if Andel had arranged for the promised grocery delivery (bless her, she had), made an omelet for dinner, and with a full stomach, flumped onto the couch to kick off his shoes and watch bad television. The dishes could wait a few minutes.

Despite the restless itching in his limbs, he fell asleep during a *Gunsmoke* episode.

He woke up half-sprawled on the sofa with a wicked crick in his neck and his right arm numb from being stuck under the structural collapse of his body. Light streamed through his floor-to-ceiling living room windows, but the quality of light was more brazen that it should be. *Morning?*

A groan and a barked shin on the coffee table later, he staggered to the kitchen. Nine a.m.

When he reached over to fill the coffee carafe

with water, he froze. The dishes he'd left to soak in the sink had vanished.

Chapter Five
Montrose in Manhattan

"I know it sounds like I'm losing it, Andel. Maybe I am." Taro swallowed hard to keep his voice from cracking. He'd been back in Manhattan for a week and still had no answers. Yes, he should've called his parents, but he couldn't yet. Not until he could tell them... something. "But it's this or admit that I need to be committed."

Andel cracked her gum a few times on the other end of the line. Easy to picture her thinking, and Taro hoped she wasn't considering calling an ambulance for him.

"Did you see a doctor, Mr. Torres? Not a shrink but for, you know, a sleep study or something. My cousin used to sleepwalk and get into all sorts of crap."

Taro sank onto the window seat's cushion. She didn't believe him and wouldn't help. Luka had sounded skeptical when he called too, but at least he'd helped Taro find a doctor in Manhattan. He'd never bothered to switch doctors when he moved. "I did. Other than telling me I have trouble falling asleep—can't imagine why—they said there's nothing wrong with my sleep patterns."

"Okay, look. I didn't tell you this, all right?"

Another gum smack. "But I might know a guy."

"What kind of guy?"

"Looks into ghosts and crud like that." She must have heard his tiny sound of dismay since she hurried on. "Oh, don't worry, Mr. Torres. He's very into sciency stuff. Not some publicity starved reality show wannabe. His name's Jack Montrose."

"So you do think it could be a ghost? Maybe ghosts?"

"Look, Mr. Torres, I'm not saying I believe in them or not. But Jack's honest. He'll tell you if it's not."

Now *that* was an odd and convoluted statement of faith. Taro wasn't certain what he'd hoped for. A wise and ancient *bruja*? A ghost expert from one of the churches? "All right, Andel. Can't hurt to have him come over, right? Thank you."

Jack Montrose. The name had a strong, official sound to it. Even if he didn't have a clue regarding what was going on, maybe he would be a Really Nice Guy, and there would be conversation, and...

"And you're getting way ahead of yourself again," Taro muttered. "Like you always do."

* * * * *

At a quarter to four, fifteen minutes ahead of

the scheduled appointment, the doorman called up to say Taro had a Mr. Montrose asking to see him.

"Yes. Of course. Thank you. Um, send him up, please?" Taro wanted to smack himself for sounding so nervous, but he wasn't used to the whole door-security thing yet, and Montrose would be his first real guest. Neither Andel nor the movers really counted. He hurried to put on some coffee, knowing his guest would be delayed by elevator rush hour. Then he paced the living room, rearranging pillows for no good reason, wishing he hadn't agreed to this.

It wasn't that he didn't like people. He did. New people in his space still made him nervous. Sometimes people he knew well still made him nervous. Power-save introvert, that's what Luka called him. He was "on" when he had to be, turned "off" the moment people left him in peace, and occasionally suffered shorts and power outages during which he couldn't interact successfully with people at all.

One of those shorts flipped his extrovert breakers to the off position when he opened the door.

"Mr. Torres?" The scarecrow in the doorway extended a hand in greeting and gave his a perfunctory shake. He patted down several pockets, both shirt and pants, before he found what he wanted with a little sub-vocal *aha* and handed Taro a business card. When Taro stood there staring at it, the scarecrow eased around him into the apartment. "Would like to poke around a bit. Then have you tell me everything that's been happening. Or we could talk first before examinations. Really doesn't matter. The order that is. Long as I'm set up before dark. But we have time..."

"Phillip." Taro finally found his voice as he stared, shell-shocked, at the business card.

Montrose glanced up from an instrument he'd been running over the sofa, bright gray eyes blinking at Taro as if he'd surfaced from a dark tunnel. "Sorry?"

"We can talk in a moment. Your card says *Phillip "Jack" Montrose.* Is Jack your middle name?"

"No middle name." Montrose went right back to scanning, free hand ruffling his straw-colored hair into even messier spikes.

"Then why—?"

"What? Oh. I like Jack. Jack can be anyone. Anything. Pirate. Time traveler. Singer. Giant killer. Pumpkin king. Paranormal researcher." Montrose paused to shoot Taro a crooked grin. Then he twitched a shrug and went back to his readings. "Phillip's an accountant. Or a snooty trust-fund baby. Why are you named after a root vegetable?"

Taro needed three tries to find his voice. "I'm not."

"Taro? Big purple edible root. What poi's made of?"

"Oh. No." Taro finally had the presence of mind to shut the door. "I mean, yes to taro being a plant, but it's short for Lautaro. My name, not the vegetable. And *I* was an accountant. "

Phillip-who-preferred-Jack-for-reasons straightened. Mostly. Even slouched, his head came precariously close to the top of the kitchen doorframe. "Lautaro. Great name. From where?"

Taro tried to smooth out the frown he knew he was wearing. Here he had been expecting Van Helsing, and Andel had sent him Ichabod Crane. "It's Chilean. Not that we're from Chile. Dad's family is Mexican and Mom's from Germany. They just really admired the historical Lautaro."

"Fine... good..." Jack returned to watching his meter. "Not prying. Sometimes certain phenomena attach to ethnicities. Maybe. Making a study of it, anyway. Floor plan of the place? Though dimensions work if you know. Cubic meter calculations. Ten-foot ceilings?"

Taro's heart started to sink, and its weight pulled him down to sit on the sofa. The man was starting to come off as a crackpot and probably couldn't help at all. "What... I don't mean to sound rude, but what are you doing?"

"Hmm?" Jack's head jerked back up again. "Is it time for talking? Good idea. You're the client, after all."

He plunked down on the other end of the sofa, all knees and elbows, and turned an arc-light smile on Taro. "So. Tell me how it started, Mr. Torres. Moved items? Keys you couldn't find?"

"Taro, please." Taro fidgeted with the hem of his shirt cuff. Even if Jack was a charlatan and a nutcase, he could easily conclude that Taro was a bigger nutcase. "It started in Germany. And you didn't answer the question."

"Germany? Then it moved here?" Blond eyebrows drew down over Jack's beaked nose.

"Yes. Sort of. It's followed me through several locations. You still didn't answer the question."

"What quest—oh! Right. Meter." Jack held it out, his long fingers gesturing at the meter as he spoke. "Just an electromagnetic field gauge. Nothing spooky strange. Lots of models you can get these days. It's a nice one. Reads up to eight gigahertz."

Taro stared at the box with its digital screen and orange ball on top. "It does look nice. But that's still not an answer, really."

"Of course it—oh. Yes. Sorry." Jack tapped the gauge against his palm and sat back, still slouched with his knees poking out so it looked like a rumpled stork had crash-landed in Taro's living room. "Thing about *hauntings*—" He stopped for air quotes. "Strong EM fields mess with tired brains. Sometimes. Create hallucinations of cold spots and hovering, misty figures. Some people even hear voices."

"Is that why it happens at night?"

"One reason. Not saying all phenomena are EM field things, but ruling it out first? Always good."

"All ghosts end up being magnetic fields, then? Someone's neural misfires?"

"Not all. Ninety-five percent have regular, everyday explanations." Jack shot him one of those mad grins. "One lady had an African gray parrot. He'd escape from his cage at night. Throw everything off her desk. Re-lock the cage behind him when he climbed back in."

Taro snapped his mouth shut. "Wow."

"Angry with her for taking a full-time job. Less time for him." Jack set the gauge on the coffee table and took out a dog-eared notebook. "The other five percent make life interesting. So. Why do you think you have ghosts?"

Slowly, carefully, to make certain he didn't miss details or tell anything out of order, Taro started with the small items he'd noticed being cleaned or put away in Marburg. He kept the retelling of his own fear to a minimum, partly because he still felt ridiculous and partly because only facts would be helpful and relevant.

"So I think I have a... a poltergeist." A sour ache settled in his stomach as he admitted it. "And it's following me. Or maybe I'm suddenly attracting poltergeists everywhere I go."

Jack tapped his pen in a rapid-fire staccato against his notebook. "Have you considered, and not just cookware alarms across your doorway or a half-baked sleep study, that it might be you?"

"Of course I did." Taro stared at the floor, willing himself to hold together. This man didn't believe him. Why should he? "That's what the pots and pans were for. I just thought I was tired and stressed and doing things I couldn't remember."

"Cameras?"

"What?"

Jack used his pen to point at the corners of the room. "Security system? Cameras? Would show if it was you."

"Oh. No. This condo did come with cameras, but I had them taken out. It just seemed a little creepy. The other three properties were older and didn't have cameras." Taro managed a sideways glance, but Jack was craning his head around the room, apparently searching for something. "I'm sorry."

"Expensive place. Unusual not to have them, Mr.—ah, Taro." Jack unfolded from the sofa to resume his slow pacing and meter-reading around the room. "Could've installed one anytime. Any of your properties. Hired someone to watch."

Taro's face heated so fast his eyes burned. "I didn't think of it."

Jack muttered something as he checked

behind the television cabinet. He got down on his hands and knees, contorting to look up at something back there so his voice came out muffled and strained. "Just a guess. Either came into money recently or lost someone who took care of things for you?"

"That's... I don't think that's really any of your business."

"Pretty much everything is in these PPS's." Jack rose from the floor, unfolding limbs and torso like the arm of a cherry picker.

"In... what?"

"Possible paranormal situations. Not solving murders. Still playing detective though. Withholding information prevents a quick resolution."

"Only my family knows."

Jack had reached the front closet and stuck his head in, spine contorting in seemingly impossible ways as he took readings between and beneath jackets and shelves. "That you have money? Your real estate broker doesn't?"

"No, no. It's where the money comes from that no one knows. You can't tell anyone this."

Without backing out of the closet, Jack flapped a long hand in Taro's general direction. "All covered in the confidentiality agreement. Non-disclosure."

Taro wracked his brain, trying to recall if Andel had sent him any documents. "What confidentiality agreement?"

Jack's blond spikes popped up again, and he leaned around the door. "The one you—oh, shrikes. Forgot again." He rushed over to the case he'd left in the front hallway and pawed through the contents. "Should be—aha!"

The slightly crumpled paper he smoothed out on Taro's coffee table was a concise and neatly formatted contract. *Jack Montrose Para-Investigations* charged by the day rather than the hour, and Taro had no benchmark for whether the fee was outrageous or not. Other than the fee, the contract set out guarantees for the client (money back if the case remained unsolved) and Jack (not held liable for breakage due to paranormal activity) and contained a non-disclosure clause that promised complete confidentiality.

"Want me to keep working? Wait until you've signed?"

Taro startled to find those bright gray eyes far too close, Jack practically leaning his sharp chin on Taro's shoulder. *Gray. Not green, not blue. Atlantic gray.* "Um... no, you go ahead. I'm nearly through reading. So far I don't see any problems."

"Good." Jack leaped up again. He seemed to have springs instead of joints. As he restarted his scanning, heading toward the kitchen area, he called out. "Let's back up. Tell me about family. Childhood."

Instead of trying to shout after him, Taro

signed the contract and hurried around the corner to the kitchen. "I'm the youngest brother and the only biological kid my parents had. They fostered lots of kids and adopted my three older brothers way before I surprised them. Dad worked on the mushroom farms just like his dad until he got a job at a department store. That's where he met Mom. Our house wasn't huge, but big enough for us. I didn't have any big traumas happen. It was a normal childhood, I guess. Um... I went to Penn State and got an accounting degree."

"Any odd occurrences growing up? Anything you couldn't explain? Things moved? Missing?"

Taro made himself stop and consider carefully. Had there been? Things moved without physical intervention? He'd had a couple of Star Wars action figures vanish at one point, but that had probably been their Labrador, Barney, who often ate strange things. "No."

"Still no money explanation." Jack froze, then whirled around to fix Taro with a horrified gaze. "Not drugs, is it? Cragmites. Should have asked that *before* you signed."

"What? No!" Taro heaved a breath and lowered his volume so he wouldn't squeak. "I won the Powerball. It was the biggest one yet. I've heard... stories about what happens when people go public. All the harassment and the people begging for money. We kept it quiet so no one outside my family and the lottery commission know."

"Won't breathe a word." Jack had returned to rummaging through mostly empty cabinets. "Blessing and a curse. Winning the lottery. You seem to be doing all right?"

"I was doing fine before, but I think I know what you mean. I'll probably never stop being careful with funds." *Cheap*, Craig would've said. "So I'll probably never buy tons of *things*. The freedom of movement's been the biggest change."

Jack finished with the last cabinet and closed it with a nod. "Need to set up cameras. Where should I sleep?"

"Sleep?" Taro's voice decided on a fancy crack-and-squeak combination.

"Of course. Have to set up equipment and camp here to catch your uncommonly tidy poltergeist. Early evenings? Manifestations don't happen early. May as well catch a nap." Jack tipped his head to the side, his forehead crinkling in an endearing way. "You too. You look tired."

Can't imagine why. "Oh. Um. I wasn't... expecting that. But I guess it makes sense? Does it make a difference where you sleep? I do have guest rooms for family, but the couch is a fold-out, if that works better for you. Since most of the, um, activity seems to happen outside the bedroom."

Jack paced around the living room, clapping his hands together softly. "Perfect. Couch is great.

Leave some bait around. Dirty some glasses. Strew some clothes."

"I'm not sure you can use that verb that way."

Instead of answering, Jack stared down into his equipment case as if it might tell him things. Stork-scarecrow, yes, but there was a strangely self-contained grace about him, though grace*ful* wasn't at all the right word. More of a quality of completeness, an impression Taro couldn't explain even to himself. That Jack was just himself and didn't hide it. He found it oddly compelling.

A bit unsettled by that thought, Taro left shoes in the middle of the floor, tossed a hoodie carelessly over a wing chair, and drank soda out of three separate tumblers in the kitchen while offering a fourth to Jack. The thought of having a stranger in his space wasn't entirely comfortable, but Jack wouldn't be intruding on his personal space with him setting up camp in the living room and Taro shut up in the bedroom.

He said goodnight to Jack, whose mad grin hadn't dimmed a single watt, and retired to his bedroom, anticipating another restless night. As he settled under the blankets, he winced at the clanks and clatters from the front room. Taro hoped those were all *normal* equipment setting-up sounds.

Chapter Six
Data in Queens

Several thudding crashes woke Taro from a late-night television doze. One of the PBS stations had been playing a *Blackadder* marathon, and he'd nodded off somewhere during the Regency era.

Jack had gone quiet after his initial set up, though his lanky frame artfully arranged on the sofa bed was too full of tension to fool any self-respecting ghost into thinking he was sleeping. At least that was Taro's impression when he'd gone to the kitchen for a glass of water. Strange, twitchy lightning rod of energy, Jack Montrose.

Having another person in the condo did alleviate his fears, and he'd been determined to stay up this time, listening for the clink of glasses, for the start of *something*. Naturally, he'd fallen asleep.

The fear slammed back into his chest with those thuds. He hesitated with his hand on the bedroom doorknob. Something *bad* was happening out there, and all his instincts screamed at him to not to open the door. Problem was, this time there was someone else out there who might be experiencing the bad things. Alone. Frightened as Taro was, he still couldn't abandon another human being.

He pulled in a huge breath, yanked the door open, and rushed down the hall to the living room. "Jack! Are you—"

The question choked off at the base of his tongue when he flicked on the lights and spotted Jack crumpled face first on the carpet, one long leg draped awkwardly over a round ottoman. Taro hurried across the room, turning on lights along the way.

"Jack? Are you all right?"

He got a muffled groan in response, not at all encouraging. Jack rolled and his leg flopped to the floor with another thud. *There's blood. Shit, shit, mierda, there's blood.* Taro swallowed hard and managed two slow breaths before he could unfreeze his feet for those last three steps.

"Can you hear me? Jack?" Taro knelt and gripped Jack's shoulder, relieved when those oversized gray eyes fluttered open.

"Hello, there," Jack whispered. "Aren't you the prettiest?"

Taro snatched his hand back, his face sunburn hot. "Um, are you okay?"

"Oh." Jack blinked and his eyes started to focus as he dabbed his sleeve against his nose. "Sorry. Yes. Probably fine. Managed a nice face-plant there."

"What happened?"

"Shuffling noises. Your jacket was gone. Glasses started clinking in the kitchen. Tried to sneak over and see what was happening. Couldn't have been you. Still in your room."

"How could you be sure? I mean I wasn't in the kitchen, but I could've been."

Jack's grin was only half its usual strength, definitely more chagrined than manic. "Your door squeaks. Tiny bit of WD40 would take care of that —"

"I'll keep it in mind." Taro cut off what sounded like the start of a home repair lecture and hurried to the bathroom for a washcloth. Once he had it thoroughly wet and wrung out, he went back and handed the cold washcloth to Jack. "For your nose. I hope it's just a nosebleed. You were at clinking glass."

Jack sat up slowly. The washcloth pressed to his nose exaggerated the nasal quality of his voice almost to cartoon character levels. "Right. Tiptoed to the kitchen. Could've sworn I knew where the ottoman was. Tripped over it."

Taro shook his head. "I thought something horrible was happening out here. Are you sure you're all right? Is your nose broken? Do we need to get you to the ER?"

"Would be a tragedy. Breaking my regal schnoz. Pretty sure it's fine. Just a little bigger for a few days." The corners of Jack's eyes crinkled. "Want to see if we've had a visitation?"

Out of courtesy and because it seemed impossible that *something* wasn't broken, Taro helped Jack to his feet. Jack hobbled a little and retained a grip on Taro's shoulder, but all his appendages apparently worked. A sudden vision of having to stuff straw back into Jack's shirt, like Dorothy with the scarecrow, made Taro choke on a laugh. From the look Jack shot him, turning the laugh into a cough hadn't fooled either of them.

In the kitchen, Taro's amusement died a swift, messy death. All of the glasses they had left artfully scattered across the counter had vanished. Jack pulled on a latex glove from his pocket and eased open the cabinet door. He picked the glasses up one after another to examine the rims and the bottoms, though Taro knew what he would find. Clean. All of them sparkling clean and dry.

"Well, now." Jack's whisper shook with obvious excitement. "Isn't this interesting?"

"It's just like all the other times," Taro said, fidgeting with his pajama cuffs. "Did you see anything?"

"No, but cameras were in the right places. Should take them back to the lab and—"

"No." Taro flailed for words while Jack regarded him with raised eyebrows. *I feel terrible that you got hurt investigating my ghosts, and I don't want to be alone here.* "Um, you just had a bad fall and... your nose is still bleeding. You could stay. Since you really should rest. I... you need some ice."

Jack took the washcloth away from his nose

and winced as he examined it in the mirrored shine of the refrigerator. "Not a bad idea. All right. Some sleep and lab in the morning. Sure you don't want me to start on analysis?"

"It's fine. I've waited this long. I can wait until we've had coffee. And bagels. There definitely have to be bagels."

Blond eyebrows threatened to vanish into Jack's hairline. The grin crept back slowly. "Offering to make me breakfast?"

"Ha! Um, yes. Not like that. But you're here and I'm your host..."

"Sorry, sorry." Jack closed the cabinets gently. "Technically, it's a client-to-tradesperson thing. But nice of you. Ice?"

When he'd settled Jack as comfortably as possible on the sofa bed with an ice pack and extra blankets, Taro wandered back to bed. The *visitation*, as Jack called it, was probably over for the night. Safe to sleep. Having someone in the next room certainly helped.

* * * * *

The next morning, Jack was plowing into his fourth bagel half, a frown of concentration wrinkling his forehead, when Taro finally interrupted his camera perusal.

"What are you seeing? Anything?"

Jack's head jerked up, though he raised a

finger to ask for a moment as he dealt with the huge bite he'd taken. His appetite certainly belied his physique—one of those men his mother would claim had either "a hollow leg or a tapeworm."

"Not yet," Jack pointed to the cameras. "Too dark. Don't expect much without all the filter software."

"Then why check them all?"

Jack took a gulp of his milk-and-sugar drowned coffee, back to staring at the camera footage. "Never know. Thought I saw movement on one. Wouldn't feel right not to check."

Taro nodded sagely as if he understood and spread cream cheese on another bagel. He slid it over to Jack before he had finished devouring, deftly replacing the empty plate with the full one. Jack murmured a thank you, eyes glued to the footage.

"What should I do today?" Taro cleared his throat. "Any way I can help?"

With a rapid series of blinks, Jack resurfaced and smiled at him. "You can come with me. Unless you're busy. Should've asked that first."

"I don't have anything planned. But I don't know anything about all this. How would me tagging along help?"

After tackling another crocodile bite of bagel, Jack said, "It doesn't. Not the tagging along. But if there's something, might be fun to see, right?"

"Only if it turns out to be the ghosts of fluffy

kittens." Taro sipped at his own mug of still-recognizable-as-coffee and heaved a shaky breath. "Okay, no. You're right. I'd rather know instead of sitting here, waiting for you to call."

"You'd never have to wait long."

That sounded suggestive. Maybe. He's strange but in a good way. Even attractive, in a weird, stretched-out Danny Kaye sort of way. Do I want it to be suggestive? I don't even know... I'm being stupid. I don't even know for certain if he's gay. Though he did call me pretty. Really, really stupid. "Well, good."

There was none of the morning-after awkwardness of trying to rustle up soap, packaged toothbrush, and razor. Jack came prepared, since, as he cheerfully admitted with that ambiguously suggestive smile, he often stayed the night with clients.

"You do know how that sounds, right?" Taro asked with an exasperated laugh.

"Yes." Jack tapped the end of Taro's nose with his toothbrush case and disappeared into the guest bathroom with a wink.

You can't. You know you can't. He won't understand. Yes, Jack showed signs that he was gay or bi. Yes, Taro had long gotten over thinking of himself as "abnormal" or "frigid." But he'd yet to meet a man who really got it, who didn't think he was a challenge, a sexual nut that they could crack as long as they worked hard enough.

He was who he was. Even if Jack was remotely interested, he wouldn't be for long without the sex part of a relationship. Even knowing all that? Taro's heart insisted on a budding crush, for no better reason than an infectious energy and a quirky smile, the beginnings of a crush on a scarecrow crackpot who hunted ghosts with gauges usually reserved for telecom technicians.

"Gah! Idiot." Taro stalked to the bathroom to hurry through his own morning routine, though he cleaned up around the sink and put everything in its place with extra care so the OCD poltergeists wouldn't invade his bedroom.

Of course, he was probably deluding himself that Jack had even hinted at being interested. Taro wasn't any great find: small enough that most of his female acquaintances didn't need heels to be taller; slender enough that people always stuck him in the middle of a sedan's back seat like a little kid. Too old to be a twink, he was just tiny now. Tiny Taro Torres. Alliterative names were hell on kids sometimes.

Taro grimaced as he pulled a white hair from his brush. Those were an ever-more frequent occurrence. He was just going to have to resign himself to being that eccentric bachelor uncle who lived alone. At least now, he could buy the nieces and nephews decent Christmas presents. No ponies or sports cars—that probably wouldn't go over well with his brothers—but more than Lego sets for the little ones or gift cards for the picky older ones.

He shoved his melancholy back into its well-worn box and finished cleaning up the kitchen while Jack packed his equipment. Cameras, microphones, and boxes with gauges and dials all went into cases, then into Jack's black carryall. Despite his twitches, his movements were efficient and practiced, as if he did this every day. Maybe he did.

Taro perched on the arm of the sofa to watch the packing. "How long have you been at this?"

"Since college."

Again, not an answer, since Jack's expressive face could have put him anywhere between twenty-five and forty-five. "You have a degree in... paranormal activity?"

"Civil engineering."

"Because that's not counterintuitive or anything."

Jack must have caught the sarcasm. His head jerked up, the sudden movement obviously painful, since his eyes squeezed shut and his hand went to his nose. "Right. Yes. True. Had a psych professor in college who was interested in the paranormal. TA'd for him. Did investigations on the side. Liked it better than inspecting bridges and interstate ramps."

"A lot less predictable, anyway. At least I'd

guess so."

"Some routine is good." Jack stood carefully, with one hand on the wall, then nodded as if his body was performing within operating standards. "But this *is* more fun than marking stress cracks. Ready?"

"How did you get here?"

"Subway." Jack winced when he picked up his bag, but when Taro reached to take it, he stepped back and clutched it tighter.

"Sorry. I won't touch it." Taro considered the sunny day versus Jack's probable headache and his limp. "Let's take a cab. I like driving over the bridge."

The crinkles around Jack's eyes indicated that he knew well-meaning bullshit when he heard it, but he was kind enough not to call Taro on it. The late summer day was gorgeous, the drive over the suspension bridge from park to park was beautiful, and Jack fell asleep despite his consumption of what had surely been near-lethal quantities of sugar and caffeine.

Taro had been expecting an apartment on a busy street, maybe with a broken security door and a poorly lit stairwell, so he had to ask the cabbie to confirm the address when they pulled up to a neat, semi-detached town home in North Corona. Maybe not the best neighborhood in Queens, but the houses on Jack's street were well kept.

He nudged Jack with an elbow. "We're here."

"Wha—" Jack twitched upright, one arm flailing before he caught himself. "Oh, good. Come on in. Excuse the housekeeping."

After settling with the cab driver, Taro trotted after his investigator, amused that the first floor at least was orderly and clean. Jack had already started up the stairs.

"Juice and water in the fridge. Some leftover cheesecake too, probably. Unless I ate it. Come on up to the lab when you're ready."

Out of curiosity, Taro checked the fridge. A few sad oranges, an army of condiments. No cheesecake. The way Jack ate, that wasn't shocking. He grabbed a couple of waters and followed the thumps and thuds of footsteps and furniture to the room at the top of the stairs. Here the neat rooms gave way to riotous disorder. The dimensions indicated this had probably been the master bedroom, though any resemblance to a bedroom of any sort was lost under a tangle of monitors, wires, and scattered electronic components. A laptop denuded of its housing lay on a tray table like a slain and partially disemboweled dragon. A regiment of fans of different sizes scattered another surface, wires sprouting impotently in the air like crops of the computer apocalypse.

Jack sat in a cheap rolling desk chair too small for his lanky frame, one foot propped on a milk crate while he unpacked camera after camera and carefully plugged them into bits from the wire jungle.

"Is it safe to come in?"

"Just watch the surge protectors. And that pile of printouts."

The surge strips bristled under every stick of furniture, waiting to pounce. Taro eased in carefully until he stood behind Jack, who now had his phone held between ear and shoulder, his fingers flying over two keyboards set in front of him.

"Lena? Yeah... Mmhmm... Could you? Just to... Okay..."

Half a conversation was always annoying. Jack's were worse than most. Taro concentrated on the images coming up on various screens instead of trying to guess Lena's answers. Dark blurs, muddy red blobs, gray fuzzy things—*There might be a table leg in that last one. Impossible to tell*.

Jack hung up and put the phone down, frowning at the screens. He pointed to the dark blurs. "See that?"

"Um... no?" Taro squinted at the screen.

"There. Movement." Jack backed up a few seconds and let the footage run again. "By the chair leg."

"Maybe? I guess there might be... something." If he squinted hard, Taro thought he saw something move in the shadows. "What is all this?"

Jack pointed to the individual feed windows one at a time. "Normal night camera. Infrared. Full spectrum night vision. Sonar reconstruction. Roving full spectrum."

"Roving?"

"Camera's on a little robot, like a little Roomba."

"Oh. I didn't even see it."

"Under your sofa right before the little mishap."

"I'm not going to be much help here, am I?"

Jack put the chilled water bottle against his poor abused nose. "Company's nice. Don't have much these days. But Lena has something for you when she gets here."

"Oh. I'm glad to help, of course. But what am I helping with?"

"She'll tell you. No skewing the data." Jack leaned forward as an image dashed across the infrared feed. "There! You had to see that."

"I did see something. What was it?"

"Don't know yet. Need to mark it. Synch the feeds." Just as Jack reached for the keyboards again, all the images twitched and blinked out, leaving only static snow on the screens. Jack thumped his head on the desk. "Formics and firebugs. Not again."

"What happened? What not again?" Taro

fought an odd urge to rub Jack's back. Every line of his body screamed frustration. Maybe if they had known each other better, if they'd been actual friends, he might have been comfortable reaching out. *When was the last time I felt that close to any friend, though?*

"Some entities don't like being filmed." Jack lifted his head with a sigh. "Still, there's some footage." His shoulders twitched, and he shot Taro a bit of a smile. "Lena's car pulled up. Why don't you see her? I'll deal with this."

Taro was about to ask how Jack knew when he heard it too, the chugging of an old diesel engine. He did give Jack's shoulder a reassuring pat on his way out, just normal social contact with no weirdness attached. He hoped.

Downstairs, a smartly dressed woman was just shutting the front door behind her. Her charcoal suit and leather briefcase would have been at home in a boardroom or lecture hall, her dark short-cropped hair framing a serious pixie face.

"Hello there. I'm Lena Augustine." She offered her hand and a firm, professional handshake to go with it. "You must be Taro."

"Yes, ma'am." Taro fought against fidgeting as her dark eyes seemed intent on excavating his soul. "I'm supposed to help you, but I'm not sure with what. Jack wouldn't say."

"Excellent," she murmured as she set her briefcase on the coffee table. "How's our Jack today?"

"Frustrated, I think. Something went wrong with the cameras, it looks like. And he's probably in pain."

"Oh?" Lena's mouth tightened in a moue of concern. "Why's that?"

"Maybe Jack should tell you. I suddenly feel like I'm tattling on him."

She shook her head, chuckling as she pulled out a box, a notebook, and a folded piece of cardboard. "That's fair. Since he made it upstairs to his lab, I'll give him the benefit of the doubt and say he's probably not in dire need of medical attention. Now as to what Jack asked me to do. I'm a psychiatrist with an interest in some of the less-explored territories of the human brain, and I do some consultant work for Jack. We're going to play a little game, if you agree to it, and then I'm going to ask you a few questions. I promise to explain everything when we're done."

"All right." Taro pulled a chair around so he could sit across the coffee table from her, a little anxious as she pulled a stack of oversized cards from the box. "Are those—"

She held up a finger to stop him. "You may be familiar with the concept behind these sorts of cards, but we're going to try to go into this with as few preconceptions as possible, all right?"

Taro nodded, rubbing his palms on the thighs of his jeans as she set five cards out in front of him—a dolphin, a window, a ball, a star, and a road intersection.

"Can you remember those five things?" Lena waited for him to nod, then took the cards back. "Good. I'm going to pull out cards from the deck, concentrating on one at a time. I want you to tell me which of the designs I'm holding. When you've guessed, I'll write it down and pull the next card. I won't tell you if you're right or wrong. We'll simply keep going."

She unfolded the cardboard and set it up between them so Taro couldn't see her hands. Yes, he recalled something about cards like these, something that started with a Z, but the designs were different...

"Begin."

The idea was to test his ESP, right? To see if he could read the card through Lena's mind. He concentrated on clearing out his jumbled thoughts and guessed the first one that came to him. "Um... dolphin?"

"Next."

"Ball?"

They continued through the deck for what seemed like forever to Taro's unhappy, nervous brain. When he checked the clock on the mantel, the whole "game" had taken ten minutes. She frowned at her notebook before she looked up at him with a smile.

"Taro, have you ever had dreams that came

true?"

"No, thank goodness, or I would've taken a lot of tests in my underwear."

She laughed at that, still writing. "Have you ever had overwhelming feelings of *déjà vu*?"

"No. I mean, I don't think so."

"Have you ever heard voices when you were alone?"

Taro squirmed in his chair. "No. I'm not crazy, Dr. Augustine. Jack saw what was happening too."

"Lena, please. No one is suggesting that your issues are because of mental illness, Taro. Paranormal experiences vary widely. Have you ever had instances of emotional upset when objects moved or broke in your presence?"

That was an odd one. "No. Not that I remember."

"How would you describe your childhood?"

"Mine? I was a pretty happy kid. My parents are great. I have three older brothers. Ten-to-twelve years older. They've always been kind of protective. Nothing really bad ever happened to me."

"Would you describe yourself as happy now?"

"I don't... know." Taro hesitated, tracing the corduroy lines on his chair arm. "So much has changed. I guess it's all too new right now."

She patted his arm. "Thank you, Taro. We're finished. I'm not here to upset you." When she sat back, she leaned toward the stairs and shouted,

"Jack! Are you alive up there?"

There was a thunder rumble overhead as a wheeled chair rolled across the floor, followed by the unholy trample of Jack rushing down the stairs in such a way that Taro wasn't sure if he was running or falling. He breathed a sigh of relief when Jack appeared upright and grinning.

"Lena!"

"Good grief, Jack. What happened to your nose?"

"Took a tumble. Not important." Jack flapped a hand toward the items on his coffee table. "How'd it go?"

Her smile was just shy of grim. "Taro has managed the impossible. I've never seen anything like it."

Jack's eyes widened, which should have been an impossibility. "He got them all right?"

"He got them all wrong. Every single one, which should be a statistical impossibility."

"Oh." Taro twisted his hands in his sleeves, wishing he could melt into the floor. "I'm sorry."

"Not a failing." Jack stumbled forward a step, one hand on the wall, the other pressed to his head. "Give me a second."

"Come sit down." Lena pointed to the nearest chair. "Taro, some ice and some aspirin, please?"

As he hurried to the kitchen, Taro caught sight of one of the few pictures scattered around the living room. Most were of an older couple, probably Jack's parents, but the one on the mantel was a clear indication that Jack was gay. He was smiling, down on one knee at the feet of a dark-haired man. There was a ring box in Jack's hand, but this was the only visible picture of the apparent husband or fiancé.

Taro returned, juggling water, ice, and the aspirin bottle that had been sitting conveniently— or worrisomely—by the coffeemaker. Jack had his head back to let Lena examine his nose, so Taro set everything down and resumed his seat, feeling like an interloper from several angles.

"You've managed not to break it, but I'd suggest not using your nose to break your falls in the future," Lena said as she handed him the ice.

"Not what I was going for." Jack cracked an eye and pointed to Taro with his free hand. "Statistical anomaly."

Lena gathered up her cardboard divider and her cards as she spoke. "I believe Taro has some strong, suppressed ability. The fact that he was able to guess wrong *every* time tells me that he had the answer for some of the cards—perhaps the majority, though we can't know that—and his subconscious deliberately supplied the incorrect choice. And what did you uncover in your lair upstairs?"

"Someone doesn't like being filmed. All the footage blinks out at three minutes in." Jack kept his head back but moved the ice so he could regard Lena with one mad gray eye. "But the independent mics kept going. Footsteps barely registering. Something small, numerous, and possibly physical."

Taro stared at him. "I don't see how that could be. Maybe in one house, but in four of them? It's —whatever *it* is—following me, how exactly?"

"Luggage?" Jack suggested, and it took a moment for Taro to realize he was entirely serious.

"I don't understand what you're suggesting. That I have mice with obsessive cleaning habits? Maid-service termites? Who sneak into my luggage, no matter how hasty an exit I make?"

Jack sat up, juggling the ice pack from hand to hand. "Mr. Torres, this is nothing I've seen before. I've seen a lot."

"Taro." Lena put a gentle hand on his arm. "I don't think Jack's ready to suggest anything yet. The data sounds very odd in this case and certainly inconclusive."

"That's Lena's *I have a suggestion* voice." Jack flopped back into his chair with a crooked grin.

"I do, and I'll thank you not to interrupt." Lena fixed him with a glare that could have peeled paint, and while Jack didn't precisely quail, he did squirm back in his chair. "I understand from Jack's texts, Taro, that this phenomenon occurred at several properties of yours. Do you have others across the globe?"

"I'm not sure how it's relevant, but yes."

"I apologize if the line of reasoning seems intrusive, but Jack did share a spare outline of the case with me. I'm going to propose an experiment. Just a proposal, and both of you would have to agree, of course. Take Jack and travel to one of your properties farthest from New York. Any one where you did *not* experience this set of phenomena. Don't take any luggage. None. Buy whatever you need there—camera, change of clothes, toothbrush. Then see if what you're experiencing happens there."

"Pretty expensive experiment." Jack's eyebrows were vanishing into his hair again.

"It's a good idea though." Taro chewed on his bottom lip. Part of him said this was a *bad* idea, even though part of him insisted that he had no problem spending time with Jack. This wasn't about his personal issues though. It was about resolving this strange haunting. "Just to see... Jack, do you have a valid passport?"

Chapter Seven
Interlude in Chiang Mai

Jack stretched his legs out in his first-class suite, twitched, and hastily pulled them back in.

"All right there?" Taro leaned out far enough to see most of Jack, fists clenched in his lap. Maybe getting the best seats hadn't been a great idea if Jack was struggling. The suites were amazing but had walls for privacy, and for takeoff they were in their separate spaces, across the aisle from each other.

"Never flown first class. Keep expecting them to toss me out."

That surprised Taro enough to delay his answer. He loosened his seat belt and leaned out farther so he could see Jack's face. "You belong here just as much as anyone else. No one even cares that we're here."

Jack stared morosely out the window. "You're a very kind person, Mr. Not-a-Root Vegetable."

"Thank you, Mr. Absolutely-Not-Named Jack." Taro wanted to go over there, but they were already turning onto the runway. "Hey. You're not scared of flying, are you?"

"Didn't used to be. Probably shouldn't watch all those episodes of *Air Disasters*."

"When was the last time you watched one?"

"This morning."

Taro laughed, glad to see Jack smile in return instead of taking offense. "That probably wasn't a good idea. It'll be fine. We'll be well fed, and you can sleep all you want. Or watch movies. Whatever you like."

Jack squirmed again, and Taro wondered how he was going to make it through the long flight. "Not used to being without my work. My tablet, at least."

We should've gotten you a Valium or something. "Just hold on over there. I'll come keep you company once we're at altitude, all right?"

Taro made sure he got a nod, though Jack's eyes were distressingly wide and glassy, before he situated himself properly back in his seat. There might have been some unhappy sounds from across the aisle as the jet picked up speed on the runway and leaped into the air. Taro didn't intend to mention them.

Finally, the fasten seatbelt sign turned off, and Taro crossed the aisle to Jack's space. These first class cabins for long flights were nothing like first class in the states. Each passenger got their own cubby with a wide seat that could fold down into a bed, three windows, a sill that acted as a side table, an entertainment center, a smaller seat for a companion across from the main one, and a hidden table that could fold out between them for dining.

Taro settled in the smaller seat across from Jack, whose pale complexion had gone waxy. He touched one bony knee.

"Jack. Look at me. You face ghosts on a regular basis. This can't be as scary. Tell me about it, then. Your work. Have you ever had a... a case, investigation that you didn't solve?"

"Never." A specter of a grin flitted across Jack's worried face. "Bound to happen someday. Statistically."

Possibly this one hung between them, an acrid, stifling thing. Taro chose to ignore it. "What was your first? Case, that is."

He kept Jack talking as the flight climbed above the clouds, and Jack obliged, even though his hands were white-knuckled on the armrests. Either he appreciated the distraction, or he didn't want to be rude, but after the flight leveled out, he unclenched his jaw far enough to talk without sounding like he was going to choke. Luckily, the attendant came around in short order.

"Mr. Torres? Mr. Montrose? Would you like some champagne? We have a Krug Grande Cuvée this flight."

"Thank you, yes," Taro answered for both of them. "And Jack—ah, Mr. Montrose—isn't feeling too well. Could he have some toast, maybe?"

She said all the proper concerned things and promised to bring toast, though she seemed unconvinced that toast and champagne were a good pairing. For a few minutes, Jack nibbled at the toast and went through an odd pattern of raising and lowering the window shades. It had been a good call though. Soon he devoured both pieces of toast and stopped fidgeting quite as much.

Halfway through his second glass, Jack had finally stretched out, wallowing in his seat. "So is it my turn?"

"Your turn for what?"

"To ask all the leading little noodly questions."

Taro snorted a laugh. "Jack! You're drunk!"

"No, no." Jack slumped in his seat a little further. "When I'm drunk, I'm all bitter and morose. This is just nice and toasty."

"Ha. Okay. Your turn, then."

Jack turned the champagne glass in his long, clever fingers. "Your condo hardly looks lived in. No photos. No evidence of another person in your life. Why's that?"

"Oh, not fair. I didn't ask you personal questions." Taro sighed, but he wasn't annoyed at Jack, just at being reminded of Craig again. "I haven't spent that much time there. A lot of my things are still in storage. My books. My pictures. And except for my family, there is no other person in my life right now."

"Because you don't want there to be?"

"Because I haven't found him yet. The right one." Taro hesitated and forged on, not sure what the hell he was doing. "Unlike you. I saw your proposal picture."

Jack's smile died. "The fake proposal, you mean."

"You were just pretending?"

"No." Jack put his glass down on the wide windowsill and stared out at the sea of clouds. "*I* wasn't pretending. I was planning a wedding, blissful, blind, and stupid. A week before the date, he told me he was trading up to a less-ugly model with a real job. He didn't say it like *that*, but that's what it comes down to. Tired of my strange hours. Met someone else, someone who happened to be hot, who would be there for him. Things like that."

A strong urge to hug him pulled at Taro, but he wasn't certain how Jack would receive the gesture. "What a horrible thing to do. I'm sorry he hurt you like that, but why would you keep the picture in plain sight?"

"It's a joke." Jack swallowed hard, tiny cracks sneaking into his words. "Did you see the little brass cannon model on the mantel too? It's aimed right at his head. I calculated the angles and trajectory."

Weird that his sentences are more complete when he drinks. "You did calculations for a toy cannon?"

"Well, yes. It's easy enough to figure out the dimensions of the ball from the size of the barrel and from there the weight of a proper cannonball that size. You have to get the speed down, of course, from the initial velocities along the x- and y-axes and calculation of the maximum height..."

Jack pulled a pen from his pocket and began scribbling equations on his cocktail napkin with lots of *v's* and *t's* and sines and cosines thrown in. Taro understood the basics, but he was amazed that anyone could keep all that in his head.

The whole napkin was covered with scribbles by the time Jack sat back with a crooked grin. "See? Easily done."

"Of course. A toddler could've done it," Taro said with a dry chuckle. "But do you think that's healthy?"

"Physics?"

"No, leaving your ex in plain sight so you can pretend to shoot him in effigy."

Jack tucked the calculations in his shirt pocket with a huff. "Well, not when you put it like that, no."

Taro chewed on his lip, wondering if he should just shut up. "You're not, you know."

"Not what?"

"Ugly. Your ex was an idiot."

Jack gave him a sideways glance, radiating wariness. "Thank you for trying to be nice. I know how I look. But... thank you."

Soon after that, Jack fell asleep, so the champagne had been just as good as a Valium. Taro plugged the airline-provided high-end headphones in to surf through the available music and arrived at the amused conclusion that Jack, for all his height and ability to plow through food like a human steam shovel, was a lightweight. Curled up in his seat, golden lashes throwing shadows on his skin, Jack looked so... vulnerable was the only word for it. Taro was tempted to move over there and hold him. There was just about room, but again, he didn't know how Jack would react, and it wasn't something one just *did*.

He had to wake Jack for dinner, which included a wonderful chicken curry amid a rather extravagant three-course service with proper wines that ended up being almost too much for even Jack to eat. Almost. Stomachs full, they chatted about New York and Jack's love of old cinema over after-dinner drinks, recommending books to each other and exchanging college stories.

At one point, Taro couldn't help a wry grin as he said, "I hate to say this, but this dinner's been better than most dates I've had."

Jack reached across the table and patted his hand. He left his hand there, resting lightly on Taro's as Jack stared out the closest window. "Thank you for helping me forget we're several thousands of feet up in a metal tube."

Taro turned his hand over to grip Jack's fingers, trying to pull his attention from the sky. "I think the alcohol helped more with that."

Time didn't quite come to a standstill, but it definitely picked up a muffled, wooly quality. Those long fingers lacing with Taro's felt better than they had a right to. If the attendant hadn't interrupted to clear the table and to ask if they wanted their beds readied, Jack might have said something else. He had leaned forward, something obviously churning behind his eyes. As it was, they broke apart quickly, obviously habit in front of strangers for both of them, and the conversation died in favor of preparations for sleep. It was quite a process. Between the attendants folding the larger seat down into a bed, making it up with sheets and blankets, and presenting the passengers with personal sets of pajamas and toiletry kits, Taro felt more like the subject of a solemn ritual than a passenger. Jack's utter delight in the proceedings only served to reinforce that feeling. Taro finished preparations for bed and was about to crawl in and find something inane on the movie playlist to lull him to sleep when Jack stuck his head over the wall of his suite.

"All set?"

Jack did a bobble-head nod before laying his probably inebriated head on top of the partition.

"Just wanted to say thank you. I'm going to feel really bad if I can't solve your ghost problem. This flight's been amazing."

"My pleasure. It's better having someone to share it with."

Jack nodded again and yawned wide enough that his jaw creaked.

"Good night, Jack," Taro said with a chuckle.

"Night." Jack's crooked smile vanished from atop the wall, taking the rest of Jack with it.

The movie Taro finally chose was a romantic comedy with a title he forgot as soon as the credits were over. In his flying bed, he had the most restful, uninterrupted sleep he'd managed in weeks.

Taro woke to soft morning lighting in the cabin and thought he should check across the aisle. Jack had curled up into an impossibly compact ball on his bed and had his head stuffed under the pillows.

"Jack, they'll be coming to put things back soon. Want to wake up for coffee?"

With a gasp as if he were surfacing, Jack jerked half upright, one arm flailing as he gazed around in troubled confusion. "Good morning?"

"Good morning. You're on a flight to Hong Kong. We're almost there. You're all right."

"Landing soon." Jack's eyes began to focus, but the troubled expression remained.

"Yes. We have to catch the connection to

Chiang Mai, but we have plenty of time."

"Talking about how many crashes happen within minutes of takeoff and landing would be a bad idea?"

"Very bad, thank you very much."

Despite Jack's anxieties, the landing and subsequent shorter flight to Thailand went off without a hitch. Even with the smooth flights and the wonderful service, Jack still resumed his attempts to become one with his seat as they descended into Chiang Mai, and conversation ceased until they were in the terminal. Flying was obviously not ever going to be one of Jack's favorite things, no matter how good the champagne.

The shadow of anxiety lifted from Jack's eyes as they cleared the Jetway, his head swiveling back and forth to examine the airport and appreciate the view of the nearby green, mist-wreathed hills. The customs lines weren't horrendous, and they soon climbed into one of the blue-and-yellow SUV cabs at the airport exit to head to Taro's villa.

"Villa? Really?" Jack's eyebrows were trying to escape his forehead entirely.

"That's what the real estate people called it. It's not some palace or anything, but it sits on its own property with a little mini-orchard. It's not nearly my most expensive property. That honor goes to San Francisco, but it's one of my favorites."

They stopped on the way to grab a decent camera for Jack and some groceries for the house, since Taro knew which shops were close to this house, at least.

He sifted through his key ring, found the right one, and unlocked the door to lead Jack into the kitchen. "I thought we should take it easy today, maybe see a couple of things. The time change is a killer. Then I'll take you over to the Night Market this evening and... Jack?"

A quick search revealed that Jack had found the door to the central courtyard. He stood frozen, gaping.

"Gorgeous. Just amazing."

"It's a great space, isn't it?" Taro waved a hand at the pool with the carved tile surround that took up most of the private inner courtyard with its wood-framed shaded nooks and hanging flowering vines. "You're more than welcome to take a swim."

"In what? Underwear?"

Taro shrugged. "It's just us. You wouldn't have to wear anything if you don't want to."

Jack gave him an odd, sideways glance. "Thank you. Maybe later."

"Fair enough. It's early here still. Can I make you some eggs or pancakes or something?"

Jack unfroze as his head twitched around. "No. Let me."

"But you're my guest." Taro spread his hands on a laugh.

"Flew me halfway around the world to this beautiful place. *I* can make breakfast."

Turned out that yes, Jack could make breakfast. He made an unholy amount of noise doing it and something of an unholy mess, but the resulting frittata was heavenly and large enough that Taro could gorge himself and still leave enough for Jack's bottomless pit of a stomach.

When Taro began to clean up, Jack stopped him.

"No, leave it."

"I can't let you clean up too. That's not fair."

"All part of the experiment. We leave the mess for tonight."

"But it'll be awful to clean up tomorrow—"

Jack held up a hand. "Sometimes you have to break some eggs."

Taro put the pan in the sink, shaking his head. "I think that might have been a joke. Barely. And it was terrible. Okay, it's hours until any ghost might show up. You want to just lounge around the pool or would you rather see something amazing?"

"Amazing now, lounge later?"

"I like how you think. Can you drive a motorcycle?"

Ever restless, Jack had wandered down the hall leading to the bedrooms. After a moment, he poked his head back around the corner. "No."

"That's all right. You can ride with me."

The moment Taro said it, he realized what an odd sight they would be, with Jack all knees and elbows, both perched behind him and towering over him. People would probably stare at Jack's height, but the thought didn't bother Taro as it probably should have. It made him smile. He motioned for Jack to follow and took him to the outbuilding that had been designed for a car, but in a busy city like Chiang Mai, a car could be a liability. Bikes and scooters zipped through the worst of the traffic, so he kept a little red Honda Rebel and a larger blue Kawasaki Versys instead of a four-wheeled vehicle.

Jack eyed the larger bike warily. "We won't be too heavy?"

"I know it's not a huge bike, but I'm short. I can't ride anything too big." Taro handed over his spare helmet. "And I don't think the two of us together weigh as much as a single linebacker."

Taro clicked the strap on his own helmet and threw his leg over the bike. "Climb on. You'll be sitting high enough to hang onto my shoulders. And you're tall enough that you can see over my head. It's perfect."

After a couple of dismayed hisses and false starts, Jack climbed on, his hands landing and readjusting on Taro's shoulders several times.

"You have to hold on better than that," Taro

called back as he started the engine. "And pull your feet up, for pity's sake. *Not* on the exhaust."

When Jack's grip finally reached serious and his size thirteen feet found the footpegs, Taro eased down the drive to the street. They zipped through the traffic, Jack yelling the first time Taro cut through lanes of cars, but all the small vehicles did the same. Soon Jack seemed to relax into the rhythm of the streets, so different from even a madhouse like New York.

Taro avoided the bulk of the old city, though he had to get from one side of town to the other. It only took a few minutes longer than cutting through the congested center would have, and soon they were on less-crowded streets, heading out into the lovely green of the western hills.

As they climbed into the waiting green, Taro realized that Jack hadn't even asked where they were going. With absolutely no reason to trust Taro, he'd flown halfway around the world, then plopped on the back of a motorcycle just because Taro had said *we're going*. A heated rainbow jawbreaker of light bounced around in Taro's stomach and insisted on lodging just under his heart, all sticky, hard, and glowing. No one had ever trusted him like this or simply let him *lead* like this. He didn't feel taller the way people sometimes did, but he felt less reduced and faded. Rehydrated by Jack's tiny, simple acts of respect.

These were dangerous thoughts, there's-acliff-coming-up-slam-on-the-brakes dangerous thoughts.

The whole ride had only been about twenty-five minutes, but Jack's climb off the bike was shaky and jerky.

Taro put out a hand to steady him. "Are you all right there?"

"Tensed up." Jack grinned as he pulled off his helmet. "It's the golden temple on the hill. The one you can see from the city. Have you been?"

"Once before. You feel up for some stairs?" Taro led the way through the car park to where Jack had a view of the Naga steps, the continuous undulating mosaic guardians that accompanied visitors along the more than three hundred steps up to Wat Phra That.

Jack had his new camera out, his eyes shining as he gazed up the seemingly endless stairs. "Wouldn't miss it," he murmured.

If Taro's last boyfriend, Craig, had been there instead of Jack, he would have been happy missing it. He would have taken a picture of the many-headed nagas and headed for the nearby funicular. *Why work so hard when you don't have to?* he would've said. Except he expected other people to do the work...

Not the time. Now was for following Jack as he bounced up the steps, stopping every few to turn back and check the view. Now was the time to enjoy this beautiful day and not worry about ghosts past or present. Despite his stop-and-start progress, Jack had flitted way ahead of Taro's plodding progress. About two-thirds of the way up, he stopped to wait and read his phone.

"Do you actually have a signal out here?"

Jack shook his head and stuffed the phone back in his pocket. "Downloaded Chiang Mai info before we left."

Taro was conscious of the people streaming up and down the stairs, but Jack made a convincing immovable object, the sandbar in the stream. "So you're all prepared now for where we're going?"

"Good to be prepared going into anything, don't you think?"

Yes. It is, though I'm usually not. Taro chuckled and continued up the stairs.

From that moment, Jack and his camera led, insisting they stop and pay their respects at the white elephant shrine and find the best views of the lush, forested hills before taking off their shoes (and in Jack's case, his socks too) at the entrance to the upper terrace to visit the golden chedi. Jack was the perfect companion for the occasion, not silent by any means, but respectful in his shutterbug fever and not prone to the less-intelligent questions Taro heard from some of American tourists. *Why are Hindu gods in a Buddhist temple?* and *Won't someone steal my shoes?* chief among them.

While Jack was busy setting up the perfect

shot of a statue of Lord Buddha with the nagas shading him, Taro found himself staring at Jack's feet as he crouched, knelt, and walked back and forth. Long and gangly like the rest of him, but sculptural in their own right, elegant and beautiful in their movements. Taro turned away as his face heated, unable to think of a time when he'd found someone's *feet* embarrassingly attractive.

At the western edge of the upper terrace, Jack suddenly froze, pointing his camera into the trees.

"No binoculars," he muttered.

Taro came up beside him, trying to figure out what he'd spotted. "What is it?"

Without moving the camera, Jack backed away from it and hooked his free arm around Taro. He pulled Taro into position in front of him, Taro's back against his chest, Jack's long fingers resting on Taro's shoulder.

"There. Look. Got it zoomed in."

Taro had to rise up on his toes with Jack steadying him to see the camera's screen. A pair of large birds fluttered on a branch in one of the nearby trees, black wings flapping, their bright bills crowned with sunset-colored protrusions.

"Beautiful," Taro whispered, though the birds were too far away to hear.

"Toucans?" Jack asked, his breath tickling at the back of Taro's neck.

Standing in what was nearly Jack's embrace, Taro had a strong urge to lean back against him, to wrap one of those long arms around him. Part of him wanted to reach for what Jack might be offering. Part of him was sorrowfully certain that any move like that would be read into and misconstrued.

"It's a hornbill." Taro ducked under Jack's arm so he could have his view from the camera back. "There are different kinds, but I'd have to look it up. Amazing, aren't they?"

"Beautiful," Jack murmured, his gaze sliding sideways to Taro for a second before he returned his attention to the birds.

After Jack had photographed most, if not every square inch of Wat Phra That, they returned to the bottom of the stairs to the car park.

This time, when the bike dipped as Jack settled himself, Taro suggested, "If it's making you nervous to just hold onto my shoulders, you can hold on around my waist. I really don't mind."

It was safer for Jack that way as they drove back down the mountain. Not that Jack wrapping long arms around Taro's waist made him smile. Not at all. At least with the face shield down, he could pretend. Back down through the forest, back toward the city, Taro decided they'd make one more stop before calling it a day. If they were only here until tomorrow, he couldn't let Jack leave Chiang Mai without seeing both a beautiful wat and one other thing.

"Where to now, boss?" Jack yelled near his ear

at a stoplight.

"Elephants."

"What?"

"Almost there."

There were plenty of places around the city catering to tourists, allowing them to have elephant experiences, and some of these were wonderful and treated the elephants well. As amazing as it would have been to walk with, feed, and bathe the elephants, those took some planning and reservations though. *Another time*.

Which meant what? That he was planning to bring Jack back here? Taro shook his head as he pulled up at the elephant preserve. He had to stop having these odd fantasies. They were here to solve a problem. Jack was, to all appearances, not the most emotionally stable person Taro had ever met, and neither of them was at a place where they should be dating, even if Jack *had* been interested. Which he wouldn't be, especially not once Jack knew.

Still, *friend* wasn't a bad thing at all, and the more time Taro spent with Jack, the more he liked him. Jack didn't disappoint, reacting to the elephants with the same wide-eyed delight with which he seemed to approach most of life's wonders. Instead of controlled elephant experiences, the preserve offered a guide and a walk through the forest to observe elephants doing as they pleased. Some of them had lived with humans for many years and were still human-acclimated. One of these approached to greet them, an older female.

Jack stood still as she touched his shoulder with her trunk. "She's amazing," he breathed.

"You can touch her," their guide offered, his eyes crinkling with amusement.

Taro wasn't about to mention it, but Jack's hand trembled as he tentatively petted dusty wrinkled skin. The guide nudged him to join in, so he did, standing shoulder to shoulder with Jack as they petted the great gray head and the elephant petted them.

"Like... a rough sort of Styrofoam, her skin," Jack murmured. "Or a pencil eraser."

"That's not a very scientific assessment," Taro said.

"Too bad."

By late afternoon, they reluctantly left the preserve and headed back into the city proper, with Jack leaning more against Taro than he was sitting up. He realized that he hadn't fed Jack all day, which he remedied by stopping at the night market and picking up some *pat kha pao.* Jack devoured most of his in hyper-focused haste, then perked up considerably as they wandered the market and finished dinner.

"Sun's setting," Jack observed when they got back to the bike.

Taro glanced over his shoulder before he

started the bike and caught Jack's frown. "Time to get us back so you can set up. Do you have everything you need?"

"Should have. Our ghost hates cameras, so more than one's a waste."

"And if nothing came with us, I guess it won't matter, right?"

"Exactly." Jack gave him a sideways glance. "You're calm. Not scared anymore?"

Taro plunked his helmet on to hide his face. "Easier to be scared when you're alone. At least for me."

When they got back to the house, Jack requested more mess, so Taro made them beachcombers with coconut milk while Jack set up his camera on the kitchen table for the best view of the counter space.

Maybe it was the rum, maybe it had been the lovely day out, but as Taro put their empty glasses in the sink, Jack reached around him to add the spoons and nuzzled at his ear.

Taro swallowed hard, frozen for several precious seconds he knew might look like acquiescence.

"Jack, I don't think..."

With a sharp intake of breath, Jack jerked back, stumbling into the kitchen island. Taro turned to ask if he was all right, but Jack held both hands up, his complexion several shades whiter than normal. "Gorns, I'm sorry. Of course.

Completely not kosher. Not appropriate."

"Jack?"

"You're my employer. Got it. Wrong. Stupid. Sorry."

Again, Taro found himself unable to speak, out of surprise and cowardice. He let Jack wander off to the bathroom without correcting his assumptions, though he did have a valid point. This was a business arrangement, and once Jack resolved the cleaning-obsessed poltergeist issue, that would be the end of things.

He retired quietly to his bedroom and shut the door so he wouldn't cause Jack any more embarrassment.

The next morning, Jack appeared to have forgotten the incident, or maybe he'd decided to pretend it hadn't happened.

"Nothing in the night," he told Taro with a triumphant grin from where he lounged with his coffee. He waved the camera as if it were a signal flag. "Not a damn thing on film. Auto shutter kept going all night. Just a sink full of dirty dishes."

"No noises? Nothing moving?"

"Not a whisper. Okay, some bird calling freaked me out around two in the morning, but nothing paranormal."

Taro poured himself a cup and leaned against the counter. "You're satisfied then that the experiment's conclusive?"

"I am."

Taro nodded. "All right. Back to New York. This really isn't a ghost, is it?"

"I have grave doubts."

Taro groaned and called the airline to book a flight back home.

Chapter Eight
Puzzling in New York

Back in Manhattan, after sleeping off some of the worse jet lag Taro had ever experienced, he called Luka to tell him he was back home and winced through a scolding about not calling their mom.

"Soon. I just... I don't know what to tell her yet," Taro insisted. "She'll worry if I give her some half-assed explanation."

"She's already worried." Luka rarely spoke in anger, but he was definitely irritated. "I've told her you've been busy and that you're fine. I'm shocked she hasn't called you already. This isn't like you."

"I'm sorry, Luk. I am. This whole month hasn't been like anything I've ever experienced. I'll talk to her soon."

"I'd come up myself—"

"No, I know. The kids are in school. They need you there. You're a good dad."

Luka let out a soft breath that might have been a chuckle. "I'm the best brother too, and don't you forget it."

Over the next few days, Jack tried what he called *alternative corporeal entity strategies* for Taro's nighttime visitors. He spread sand on the floor to try to capture shape and size of footprints. The cleaning intruders swept up the sand before he had the chance to see any marks. He tried flypaper next in an attempt to catch something, but the only thing he caught was Taro when he forgot the sticky stuff was on the floor when he came down the hall to go to bed. He tried no-kill rattraps, baiting the traps with little piles of dust and breadcrumbs. The traps were spotless the next morning and completely empty.

"All a little frustrating," Jack muttered as he sat on the floor, staring into one of the traps. "I'm so sorry, Mr. Torres."

"Don't start that." Taro patted his shoulder and handed him a bagel. "We've practically been living together for a week. You can't get all formal on me now."

"All right. Still sorry. Never took this long. Maybe you need an exterminator."

Taro sat down across from him and gently took the trap away. "Some things are more challenging than others, right? You're not saying you're giving up, are you?"

"No! Of course not."

"Good. Eat your breakfast, Jack, and tell me what we need to do next."

There hadn't been any hint, any attempt at physical closeness since that night in Chiang Mai. Not that Jack had been rude or surly, but he had taken a few steps away since they'd come back and had returned to polite and professional.

Except this morning, he's withdrawn even more. He's so defeated. I wish I could help.

After breakfast—a single half bagel, so Taro knew he wasn't feeling well—Jack packed his things deliberately, with un-Jack-like slowness, as if every movement hurt. He had been going back to his lab for a few hours every day and returning in the late afternoons with renewed zeal and energy. Now, it was as if an evil undead wizard had sucked a large percentage of his life force. Lich. That's what they called those undead monsters. Not that Taro had ever played D&D seriously. For too many years, anyway. But he did remember.

Taro knew he should have said something before Jack closed the door behind him— encouraging, inspiring—but nothing came to him. *I believe in you.* At least he could've said that. He spent the day retrieving several boxes from storage and unpacking, setting pictures of his parents and his brothers' families on various tables, organizing his books on the shelves. Every few minutes he wondered if he should call Jack to check on him.

He's a grown man. He doesn't need you fussing. Stop it.

As he reached for his phone for the fourth time that hour, it rang. *Oh, damn it. Not today.*

"Hi, Mom." Guilt settled in his stomach,

leaden and aching. He'd completely forgotten his promise to call.

"Don't *hi*, me." Taro's mother huffed at the other end of the line. "Are you back from your worldclopping?"

"Globe-trotting?"

"As if it makes a difference. You were supposed to be staying home in New York now. Or so someone told me. I thought maybe you would call. It's nice that I need to hear it from Luka that you had left the country again and came back."

"Mom, I'm sorry. Things have been a little weird. And we were only in Chiang Mai for a couple of days." Taro cringed, realizing his slip too late.

"We? Who is this *we* now? Are you carrying mice in your pockets?" The *s*'s were sharp. Her accent always became thicker when she was upset.

"No, I was there with a... a friend." The last thing Taro wanted to do was explain cleaning ghosts and Jack to his mother.

"A friend. Whom you scoop up and take to Thailand on a whim." Her nails tapping on some hard surface came through loud and clear. "It's none of my business, of course—"

That would be correct, but I can't say that to her.

"—I just hope he's nicer than that Craig

person. I never liked him."

"It's not like that, Mom. Please don't make this into—"

"Anyway, that's not why I called. Your father and I would like to see you, if you can stay in one place for a few days. Will you be there this weekend? We can meet your new young man when we come up."

"Mom, he's not..." Taro sighed. He couldn't tell his parents not to come visit. Well, he could and hurt their feelings and not be able to explain why. It was only Monday. Things would be better by the weekend. "I'll be here for a few weeks. That's fine."

"Good. Luka sounded worried. He didn't ask us to check on you, but we thought you might like some company."

"So that you could check on me." Taro shifted the phone between his ear and shoulder as he checked the fridge. *Probably should do a grocery order.*

"You've had so much happen," she said, her voice softer. "Yes. We worry."

"I'm okay, Mom. I am. I was getting a little tired and stressed out at the end of the, um, worldclopping. But it's better now. It would be nice to see you."

"All right. Say hello to your young man for us."

Taro didn't have the energy or the courage to

explain that there was no young man or boyfriend of any age. His parents had known since he was twelve that he was gay, and while that hadn't been the happiest conversation of his life, they'd always supported him. But explaining why he couldn't keep a relationship going? That was more information than anyone should have to share with his parents.

He hung up with his mom and spotted the time. *Jack should be here soon.* Assuming everything was all right and that Jack was actually coming back. *No. Professional. He would've called if he didn't feel up to working tonight.*

The light was fading, and Taro had just dialed Jack's business line when the doorbell rang. Yes, maybe he dropped the phone and ran to the door, but he wasn't ever going to admit to it. When he yanked the door open, Jack leaned against the frame with his equipment bag and a frown.

"Had a thought," he said as he stalked into the condo.

"Just one? And hello to you too."

"Hi. Sorry." Jack managed a hint of a grin. "Lots of thoughts. One that won't shut up. Where were you, exactly, when you first noticed the phenomenon?"

"Exactly? Standing in front of the cabinet between the kitchen and the dining room—"

"In Marburg."

"Yes. In Marburg. I didn't connect it to the

poltergeists at the time, but yes. Why?" Taro led the way into the living room and sank down on the sofa, hoping Jack would join him.

Jack put down his bag and paced. Slowly. "Never experienced anything before that."

"No." Taro let out an exasperated breath. "Jack, I'm not going back to Marburg. I promised my mother just this afternoon I was staying in the country for a while."

Jack held up an index finger and sank onto the largest armchair. "Right. No. There's a housekeeper, though? Took care of the house before you bought it?"

"Before... Yes."

"Could you call her? About what's been happening?" Jack slumped in the chair. "If we trace it back. Maybe there's something."

"What sort of something?"

"Not sure. But nothing just *happens*. Universe doesn't work that way. Underlying cause to everything. Should have thought of it sooner. So *stupid*. So focused on symptoms and not cause."

"She's going to think I'm crazy."

"You're her employer. Doesn't matter if you're crazy." Jack leaned forward, his hands jerking in unhappy gesticulation. "Please ask. One more route we haven't tried. Maybe she's seen something or knows something. Has to be an explanation. Something rational that doesn't involve sentient neat-freak rats from NIHM with electromagnetic pulse weapons that take out cameras."

"Jack, when's the last time you really slept?"

"Doesn't matter." Jack swallowed hard as Taro continued to stare him down. "On the plane back from Thailand, I guess. Not relevant."

"Hmm. It is. I'm not calling Frau Voss—"

"What? Why not?"

"Let me finish, Mr. Irritable." Taro moved to the ottoman in front of Jack and started pulling his sneakers off. "I'm not calling her now because it's after midnight in Germany. You're going to take one of the guest rooms and go to sleep. You look terrible, and you're not thinking straight."

"But I need to set up! I need—"

"You need to take the night off. Desperately. I'm the boss here, right? That's what you keep saying. I'm saying you need a break. We'll call Frau Voss tomorrow and see what she can tell us."

Jack blinked at him, nodded meekly, picked up his shoes, and slouched down the hallway to the bedrooms.

That was easier than it should have been. While Taro cleaned up in the kitchen, he let Jack alone, listening to the sounds from the guest bathroom and Jack shuffling back and forth. Finally, everything was quiet, and he crept down the hall to take a quick look. The first guest-room door was open a crack. Jack's clothes were strewn across the floor, as if each article from jeans to socks had simply grown too tired of adorning a human body and had leaped to an uncertain fate. The man himself was curled into a tight nesting ball under the covers with only a hint of blond hair spiking from the top.

Concern. That was why Taro had insisted Jack crash there instead of going back to his own place: concern that he was too disoriented and exhausted to make the trip back; concern that he wouldn't rest without someone making sure he did. It didn't have anything to do with wanting Jack under the same roof. At all.

Why Jack had agreed to it without a word of argument was a mystery, though the why of it didn't really matter. To prevent any visitations during the night and because clothes scattered on the floor just bothered him, Taro tiptoed in, picked up the abandoned clothes, and closed the door on his way back out.

"And don't you dare wake him up, cleaning ghosts or maid service voles or whatever you are," he said in as stern a whisper as he could manage.

He stayed up until eleven reading a forgotten mystery he'd found while unpacking, then checked on his guest before he went to bed. Jack hadn't stirred a hair, and the condo was quiet. Even with not a ghost mouse stirring and with the fear from the early visitations banished, Taro couldn't get his thoughts to settle. He kept turning things over in his brain, like where his second purple sock might have gone, whether Jack liked empanadas, what he should do about his travel schedule, and Jack, whether he should change the sheets yet, and Jack.

At around two in the morning, Taro threw back the covers with an irritated sigh. He wasn't going to sleep, and he was thirsty. *Might as well do the warm milk thing*. The frame creaked as he eased out of bed, and he winced. Extra quiet. He had to be extra quiet since he had a guest. The last thing he wanted was to wake Jack and have *him* spinning his mental wheels until morning too.

Soft, slow, he sidestepped the creaky spot at the doorway, stepped carefully on the balls of his feet all the way to the kitchen, and breathed a sigh of relief. Not a sound from the guest room. He clicked on the light, blinking against the sudden illumination, and froze.

There, by the sink. *There*, where he had forgotten to wash a sandwich plate. He couldn't quite understand *what* he saw. Shapes swarmed over the plate on hands and knees, cleaning up crumbs, washing the surface, at the rim of the plate, moving it away from the sink. Tiny... somethings. In the shock of the sudden light, they ceased movement.

Then they scattered in a staccato of tiny feet. Taro thought he caught sight of clothing—or was it fur? Hats? Ears? He couldn't be certain. His brain began to process images a moment too late.

They were gone, vanished into the cracks and seams of countertop and tiled backsplash. He may have shouted. The echo of it rang in his head. He ran to the counter and threw open the bottom cabinets one after the other. If he was fast enough...

Nothing. The fear slid back into his chest and swept his thoughts up into dust-plagued eddies.

"Taro?" Jack clutched the doorframe, wild-eyed and dressed in nothing but his briefs.

"I'm all right." Taro rubbed at his chest and sank into the nearest kitchen chair. "I'm... You know you have no pants on?"

Jack waved a hand, though he did sit down to drag a dishtowel over his lap. "What happened?"

"I saw them. Jack, I *saw* them. The not-poltergeists."

"What were they?" Jack reached across to grab Taro's arm, his voice a ragged whisper.

Taro stared at the veins in Jack's hand, the warmth and Jack's presence slowly leeching the cold moment of panic away. "I don't have even a hint of an idea."

Chapter Nine
Explanations on Sofas

Neither one of them slept again that night, though Jack did put on pants. They half-watched late-night television and tried to pin down what Taro had witnessed. The *large sentient insects* possibility didn't make him feel better at all.

The crawling feeling along his spine wouldn't let go. When the shivering became uncontrollable, he pulled the blanket off the back of the couch and wrapped himself in it.

Jack moved over to the sofa to put a hand on Taro's forehead. "You're not getting sick, are you?"

"No. I'm just... I haven't been scared at all the last few days, and now I can't get the... It's not like I even got a good look. Maybe because I didn't, I'm a little freaked out. Like before—" *Before you came.* "When I was alone."

"Hey." Jack wrapped him in a hard embrace, blanket and all. "You've been braver than any client I've had. And they had easy, physical explanations."

Taro leaned in, accepting the comfort, drinking in the warmth. "I was okay until they vanished. Maybe not okay, but not as freaked out.

The sheer *velocity*—"

"Speed."

"What?"

"You mean speed. Relative velocity is an expression of vector. The rate at which something travels, distance over time, is speed."

"Jack, this isn't really a good time for a physics lesson."

"Sorry. You're okay." Jack started to rock them, rubbing his hands along Taro's back. "And there's no bad time for physics."

"If I argue that point, I'll probably just set off another equation scribbling storm, so I'll let it go." Taro heaved a shaking breath and patted Jack's chest. His entirely bare dusted-with-blond-hairs chest. "It was just reaction, I think. Being on edge for so long."

"Yeah." Jack loosened his hold to look down into Taro's face. Oddly, instead of moving back to his chair, he stroked one of Taro's eyebrows with his thumb.

Golden warmth surrounded him with Jack holding him, touching him, but Taro's stomach still knotted up at the contact. The touching would lead to a kiss. Jack was already leaning closer. The kiss would lead to more intrusive touching. That would lead to—

"Jack," Taro whispered, wriggling backward.

"Sorry." Jack twitched away, barely missing Taro's head with an accidental arm flail. "I didn't

—um, so did you want to go to bed? No. I mean *back* to bed. Your bed. Our *separate* beds. Draks."

"I knew what you meant. It's almost morning. Probably better to stay up at this point." *Tell him. Tell him something.* Taro's fear of derision and rejection overrode his conscience though, and pummeled it into silence. Nothing came out.

Jack nodded miserably and plodded down the hall. A moment later, the shower started running.

"You, Torres, are a coward," Taro muttered to himself. Then again, when this was over, Jack would go back to his life, and Taro would never see him again. Better that way, really. It was.

When the sun rose and it felt like a decent hour to use the phone again, Taro called Helga Voss with Jack on the other phone in the bedroom.

"Herr Torres, hello! I didn't think to hear from you so soon." She sounded genuinely pleased that he'd called, but Taro heard the note of concern.

"It's nothing terrible. Well, nothing to do with the house. It does have to do with the house, but not about me coming back yet."

"You have no need to be so nervous with me." He could picture her holding up a hand to stop his nonsense. "Whatever you need to tell me, you tell me."

"I've been having a very strange problem, Frau Voss, and it started, I think it started, in Marburg. I have Jack Montrose listening with me. He's been helping with this... problem."

He went on to tell her about the clean glasses, about the certainty that he was sleepwalking, and then the surety that he was being haunted. He described everything that happened in Wales and on Prince Edward Island, and then in New York. Even his fear went into the narrative pot and all the things that Jack had tried—the cameras, the testing, and the luggage-free trip to Thailand.

"But you have seen nothing? And your ghost hunter has no answer?"

"I... Frau Voss, I saw them last night," Taro choked out.

Her voice suddenly became sharp. "What did you see?"

"I'm not sure. I was so shocked. They could have been tiny men in furred hats or some sort of strange, intelligent insects, or rodents. I just don't know."

She was so quiet Taro wondered if she'd decided he was crazy and had hung up on him.

"Frau Voss?"

"This is hard for me to say because no one believes it," she said softly. "I think that you have *heinzelmännchen*."

Taro took the phone away from his ear, stared at it, and put it back. "But... those are little gnomes. I thought. Like... like garden gnomes. My mother talked about them."

"They are drawn that way in children's books,

yes. I have never seen one."

"Then how would you know?"

She blew out a hard breath. "You do not need to see *heinzelmännchen* to know they are there. You do know the story? From Köln?"

The story was from Cologne. Yes, he recalled that much. "I don't really remember it."

"I will tell you it the short way. They say the people of medieval Köln were lazy, though it was not that they did not know how to work. It was because they would go to sleep at night, and in the morning, all their work would be complete. The housework, the baking, the sausage making, the cobbler's repairs—everything would be done. The *heinzelmännchen* would do them. The people needed to do nothing. But one night, the baker's wife was curious how all these things were done. Who was doing them. She spread dried peas on the floor to catch them. In the night, the little people came to do their work and instead slipped and slid on the peas. The woman watched it all. They were so angry at the trick that they went away, never to come back. The people of Köln have had to do their own work ever since."

Taro mulled that over. "Okay. That's familiar. But why do you think that's what's happening to me?"

"Because your house in Marburg, Herr Torres... I take care of the garden, but I have never had to clean the house. And I have been the housekeeper there for one owner or another for seven years."

You pay me to clean an empty house that does not need cleaning. She had said that to him, and he hadn't really heard. He'd made the assumption that an unoccupied house didn't need much attention. Preoccupied with other things at the time, he forgotten the conversation until her words reminded him.

"Why didn't you tell me?" Taro asked, then cut his rising voice off, pinching the bridge of his nose between thumb and forefinger. "No. That's a stupid question. I wouldn't have believed you."

"I would think not. You would have thought I was telling stories or that I was crazy."

"So do you think since I saw them, they'll go away?"

"I don't know, Herr Torres. They are far from their homeland and must have followed you for a reason. Perhaps they will vanish as they did from Köln. Perhaps not."

"Thank you. For telling me. I probably should have come to you first."

"I am sorry that they frightened you. I regret not mentioning them."

Taro said goodbye to her and called out, "Jack, did you get all that?"

When he didn't get an answer, he left the kitchen and nearly collided with Jack, scribbling madly in his notebook, as he came down the hall.

"Got it... got it. Not a manifestation so much as a first contact scenario."

A laugh surprised Taro. "These aren't aliens."

Jack glanced up from his scribbling, blinking. "Aren't they? Intelligent beings. Not human."

"But they live here with us. On this planet. They may have been here before us."

"Same rules apply." Jack tapped the end of Taro's nose with his pen. "Can't make assumptions about motives or culture. But you don't need me for that." He wandered back out again, his momentary excitement over discovery apparently deflating. "And you solved this yourself."

Taro ventured out to the living room where Jack was packing up. "I've probably been taking a lot of your time. I'm sorry. You have other clients to see, I'd guess."

Head down, in the act of tucking away his notebook, Jack stopped. It took him a full thirty seconds before he raised his head slowly to lock eyes with Taro. "Mr. Torres, I often don't have clients for weeks at a time. I do freelance drafting for more regular income. Sometimes I resolve things, like the parrot. More often than not, the phenomenon goes away on its own. In this case, I haven't accomplished a thing. I'll be returning your deposit in the morning."

Okay, full sentences when drunk and full, formal ones when really upset.

Jack unfolded his legs to stand and picked up

his case as he turned toward the door.

And he's walking out. He's upset and maybe humiliated, and he's walking out. No, no, no, no...

"Jack, wait!"

Jack hesitated with his hand on the front doorknob. "It was nice to meet you. Thank you for indulging me."

With nothing else ready in his limited social arsenal, Taro rushed across the room and plastered himself against Jack's back, arms wrapped around his waist. "You can't go like that. Not when we finally know something. Of course you did things. You eliminated what it couldn't be. You're the one who made me stop and think about all of it. Without you here, I would've been coming unglued, still thinking a ghost was chasing me, for whatever ungodly reason."

"And this. This right here." Jack patted the hand Taro had laid flat against his stomach. "Why I have to go."

Taro swallowed hard, but he didn't have any doubts about what was coming next. "What?"

"The mixed messages. The come-here, get-the-hell-back. It's hard on me, Taro. Really hard." At least Jack turned to lean his back against the door instead of leaving. "I'm not pretty. More like the Vlasic pickle stork had an illegitimate kid with a stick insect. I know. But could you have the decency to say it? 'Jack, I don't want you?'"

"But I do want you."

Jack slammed his head back against the steel door several times. "Oh, my fucking god."

No, no, no, Jack doesn't cuss. I have to fix this. Have to. "Can we sit down? Please?" Taro tugged at one of his hands, gratified when Jack came along. "I need to tell you something. It's one of those *it's not you, it's me* things. But it's not going to be what you think."

Jack perched on the edge of the sofa, as far away from Taro as he could get, eyebrows drawn in with his frown. At least he was sitting.

"I like you." Taro edged a little closer, though he didn't want to crowd Jack, not yet. "I like spending time with you. Having you here. But I can't have sex with you."

"Because I'm repulsive. Already covered this part."

Taro held up a finger. "No. I need you to listen. Really listen. Okay?" He waited until Jack gave him a hesitant nod. "It's really not you. It really is me. I'm ace, Jack. Asexual."

A bit of forehead crinkle joined the frown. "So you've never had sex?"

Oh, I wish I had flashcards for these conversations. "Virgin and asexual aren't synonyms. Yes, I've had sex. I just don't enjoy it."

"Maybe you've just had terrible partners?"

Taro rubbed both hands over his face. "Jack, please, please don't be one of *those* people."

"Not that I don't know what ace *is*." Jack

settled further back on the sofa. "But I'm confused. Why the... snuggling? Was it playing? Am I *safe* because I'm so ugly?"

"First of all, knock it the hell off with the ugly bit. I know you've probably heard it. You're not the stereotype of a hunk. So what? You're not ugly, and you have the most amazing eyes." Taro stopped for a breath, since he'd been starting to shout. "So quit it. For the rest of it, no, I don't think you really understand what being ace is. I'm not mad about that. Lots of people don't. It took me a long time to understand myself, especially since everyone insisted something was wrong with me."

Jack was chewing on a thumbnail, but he managed to get out, "People thought you were broken."

"Yeah. They did. They do. I've had boyfriends insist I was repressing some abuse from my childhood, or that there was some other trauma I wasn't dealing with. I'm not. I was a happy kid, and the most traumatic thing that happened to me was Billy Swenson calling me a fag in high school. But people keep wanting to fix me."

"I get that." Jack leaned forward, clasped hands between his knees, staring at his shoes. "The wanting to fix part. Doesn't really answer the question."

"About how I've acted with you." Even though he shook, Taro reached out to take one of Jack's long hands between his. "It's hard. Having to come out like this every time there might be a chance of... something. Because people don't understand. Sometimes they don't even try. My last boyfriend insisted that sex was a mandatory part of a relationship, or it wasn't a *real* one. I can't go through that again."

"You're doing it again." Jack nodded to their joined hands.

"Touching you? Yes. Look, some asexuals like certain aspects of sex, or under certain circumstances. A lot of asexuals still long for touch. I like being held. Holding hands. Having someone to snuggle up to in bed. I like kisses, up to a point. But it almost always comes with expectations. The other person's, that is. And when I start feeling it slide toward the expectation of more, of the whole kanoodle, I seize up. I have to step back. Disengage because I feel like I'm going to suffocate."

Encouraging, that Jack had made no attempt to pull away. Instead, he stroked his thumb over Taro's fingers. "Should have talked to you. Instead of... Did you really just say the whole kanoodle?"

"Yes. Got a problem with that?" Though he tried to sound tough, Taro couldn't help a snicker, relieved when Jack cracked a crooked smile. Finally.

"No. Taro, tell me what this is here. Just... I... Never, I'd never ask for something you couldn't give. Or didn't want to give. Or didn't like. Enthusiastically like. But what is this? This happening here?"

"I like you. A lot. You're smart and funny and a little off kilter. I love watching you drink in the world and get excited about something as simple as an equation. It feels good when you hold me. Really, really good. I guess I was hoping we could start seeing each other. Outside of this, um, case."

"Mr. Torres, you're asking me out? Shocking. Still my employer, technically."

"I'm not... Maybe? I don't mean it in a creepy, I'll-pay-you kind of way."

Jack tapped the end of Taro's nose. "Yanking your chain. You did whisk me off to Thailand. Felt a lot like a date."

"Is that a good thing? I didn't want to make you uncomfortable. It just felt so good to have someone with me. To have *you* with me."

"Loved being there with you. Especially now I know." Jack pressed the back of Taro's hand to his cheek. "Can't pretend I'm not disappointed. A little. You're hot as hell, and yeah, there was some heavy lusting going on. Still is. Not the only reason I was hoping there might be something though. Not even close. Probably why it hurt so much when—"

"When you thought I was jerking you around."

Jack did a slow collapse onto his back with his

head in Taro's lap. "This okay?"

"I promise, I'll say when something isn't."

"Biggest problem I see is the income gap, not the sex gap," Jack said as he wriggled into a more comfortable position. "Money can cause more fights than anything."

Taro leaned down to plant a soft kiss on Jack's forehead. "We'll figure it out. Right now, I was hoping you could figure out how to communicate with my stowaways slash houseguests."

"About that." Without getting up, Jack reached out and dragged his bag to him. "I have this really tiny microphone..."

* * * * *

At Jack's laboratory office the following morning, they finally had something. Apparently, the *heinzelmännchen* understood enough about cameras to interfere with their functions but not about tiny microphones.

Taro stood with his hand on Jack's shoulder, leaning in to hear the soft squeaking that Jack had enhanced enough to reveal voices and words.

"Waneem is der jung Keerl?"

"In'n Alkoon sachs."

"Heff em ni kieken."

Jack played the few sentences over and over shaking his head. "Can't make out a thing. Dutch maybe?"

After the fourth listen, it dawned on Taro. "It's *Plattdeutsch*. Low German, though that's kind of a misleading thing to call it. The dialect from the lowlands up north."

"You understand it? We should try to communicate if we can. See if there's a reason they came with you."

"I can only catch a word here and there. But I know someone who does understand." Taro squeezed Jack's shoulder. "How would you like to meet my mother?"

Chapter Ten
Answers in Kitchens

"Stay here." Jack's arm snaked out and looped around Taro's waist, pulling him tight against Jack's chest. "Don't get up."

Taro clawed at the edge of the bed, laughing and trying to get some traction. "I have to get up. My parents are coming."

"Not like you have to clean the place up." Jack buried his face against Taro's shoulder, his words drifting out in a muffled grumble. "And we could just hide in here."

"Tempting." It was in some ways moose-tracks-sundae tempting. "But it's my *mom*."

They had spent another evening together after Jack had finished some contract work, and he had demonstrated that when he wasn't working, he wasn't part stork at all. He was part cat, happy to curl up on the sofa with Taro and watch movies. After popcorn and the second movie of dubious quality, he'd been happy to curl around Taro in bed as well, no pushing for more, no wandering hands.

This morning, Taro wasn't as sure. Jack's morning erection nudged at his hip, and this insistence on impeding his progress out of bed made him uneasy.

"Jack."

With a grumbling sigh, Jack let go and rolled onto his back. "Playing. Teasing. Not trying to molest you. ROEs. Think I could have some?"

"ROEs?"

"Rules of Engagement."

Taro stared at him. "I don't... have those."

"Never mind." Jack scooted around him to reach his pants, carefully hung up on the chair to avoid *heinzelmännchen* interference. "Better get home."

"You don't have to."

The look Jack shot him was a mix of hurt and skepticism. "Your parents. Not meeting them without something decent to wear and a shave."

Off balance and distracted, Taro let him go, though in the shower a few minutes later, he wanted to kick himself. He had to stop that. Stop shutting down when he didn't have answers right away. *I'm sorry. I made you feel bad again.* Maybe even, *Can I think about that for a while?*

So far, despite his own insecurity issues, Jack had been patient. But rules? Taro was used to rules coming from other people, to all the compromises being his. It was just going to end up the way it always did with sexual males. Eventually, Jack would start to push the boundaries, and the anxious thoughts would start. Could he do it? Was he responding in the right way? Maybe if he just finished things quickly so it could be over?

He didn't want to go through that again, not even for Jack. Maybe this would end just as badly as every other relationship. Maybe it wasn't worth trying again.

"Getting ahead of yourself. Again. Always," Taro muttered to himself as he wandered to the kitchen. "Like the story about the silly family and the ax stuck in the ceiling that might fall and kill someone someday."

At least it looked like his nightly visitors had received his invitation. The plate with the pyramid of miniature brownies was now clean and in its spot in the cabinet. The tiny plastic thimblefuls of juice had been emptied and washed out, the little regiment of colored thimbles lined up neatly on the counter. His invitation, in words he'd had to look up online, handwritten in the smallest letters he could manage, had several neat little marks at the bottom, which could've been agreement, or they could've meant *fuck off, giant*. Impossible to say.

He hoped Jack had eaten, since he'd run out before Taro could feed him. The sheets had to be changed. These had been on the bed since they'd met, and Jack was going to start to wonder about his hygiene. The towels too, and he needed to unpack the rest of his suitcases. Living in the same few changes of clothes that Jack had seen already was getting old.

His bakery delivery came, bagels, bread, and the pastries for his parents' visit that afternoon. *Maybe I should put something in the slow cooker for lunch. Was Jack coming back for lunch?*

Halfway through stuffing the sheets and towels in the laundry machine, he stopped. When had such a huge percentage of his thoughts started to center on Jack? How did this happen in less than two weeks? Not that he could pretend it wasn't happening. Jack had wriggled his way deep into Taro's brain, and his absence now felt strange and disorienting, as if the condo had developed a Jack-sized hole.

No more compromising for anyone. He had to keep that in mind, no matter how his heart felt. That was the important part, and he had to stick to it this time. No more feeling like he was being slowly backed into a corner. No more feeling broken because of someone else's preconceived ideas.

Jack didn't come back for lunch, which made Taro worry that he was only eating sugar. He had some of the chili himself and put the rest in the fridge for later, just in case. With the coffee maker burbling, he pulled out a serving tray and cut danishes precisely in half, just in time for the doorbell to ring at exactly two o'clock.

He flung the door open to reveal his parents arm in arm, just over five feet tall, the pair of them, and still wedding-cake-couple adorable after so many years. "Mom! Papi!"

For a moment, he let his adult status melt away as he flung himself into their waiting arms, their youngest child, their baby boy. He blinked back sudden inexplicable tears as he led them inside. "I'm so glad to see you. Come on and see the place."

"You look tired," his father said as he handed over his coat.

"Where are your bags?"

His mother swept right in. "We have a hotel room, since we didn't want to intrude on your new arrangements. Well, where is he? This new one."

"He's not here yet, which gives us time to talk, and his name's Jack, Mom, so you won't call him *the new one* when he gets here."

She frowned at him, and he realized the white hairs had begun to overpower the blonde ones in his mother's bushy eyebrows. "Jack? So he has only one name, like Cher?"

"No, I don't think he's much like Cher. Though he's tall." He strode to the kitchen as he talked, not even bothering to ask them to sit down. He knew they would follow. "His name is Philip Montrose, but he likes people to call him Jack."

"Hmph. He sounds like some stockbroker. Or a lawyer. Is he a lawyer?"

"No, he's not." Three trips from kitchen to living room with trays and extra hands to help had all of the coffee accoutrements and pastries set out before Taro continued. "What he does is part of why I asked you to come visit a little early. This is going to all sound strange, but I have several people you can check with if you need to verify certain points." He held up both hands when his father made a sound of protest. "I know you won't, but I also don't want you worrying that I'm having some sort of breakdown."

One more time—in a more organized and detached fashion, since he'd had some practice by now—he told the whole story to his parents beginning in Marburg. While their expressions did move more and more into the concerned spectrum, they only asked two questions as he neared the end: "Did he help to clean up?" from his mother about Jack and the kitchen experiment in Chiang Mai, to which he could honestly answer yes, and "Are you sure they weren't mice?" from his father about the *heinzelmännchen* sighting.

"Even if they are mice, Papi, they're awfully smart, organized mice who speak, and I'm hoping to be able to talk to them. See what they want. But that's what I need you guys here for."

His mother put her coffee cup down. "How so?"

"Mami," he murmured his childhood name for her. "They speak *Plattdeutsch*."

"Ah." She picked up her coffee again, taking a careful, polite sip. "It's been a long time. Your oma died so many years ago."

"I'm just asking you to try. Please. You have to remember more than I do."

More normal conversation took up the rest of the afternoon, from minor criticisms of Taro's household arrangements—*You don't have an ironing board?*—to questions about Jack, many of which Taro was embarrassed not to be able to answer. He didn't even know if Jack's parents were still alive, for pity's sake.

Around four, Taro covered up the remaining pastries for Jack to dig into later, and his mother began rummaging in the kitchen.

"What are you looking for, Mom?"

"I should get dinner started, don't you think?"

"Oh. No, Jack sent a message. He's bringing something over."

She arched an eyebrow at him. "He cooks?"

"At least some things. He said it was only polite, since I've fed him so many times." Taro hoped he didn't sound defensive, but he found himself *wanting* to defend Jack rather than feeling forced to defend him.

"Hmph. Well, that's already better than your last one."

Jack arrived soon after, arms loaded down with bags and one of those thermal carriers for baking dishes.

His grin was as bright as ever when Taro opened the door, though there might have been a hint of panic in his eyes as he whispered, "Are they here?"

Taro had hoped to give Jack a few words of reassurance, but his mother swooped in like the social hunting kestrel she was. "This must be Jack. He *is* very tall. What do you have there, young man?"

"Ah, lasagna?" Jack found himself unburdened before he could either step inside or protest. "It should still be warm," he called after her, eyes wide in shock.

"Hi." Taro tried not to laugh as he gave Jack a peck on the cheek. "My mom and dad, Manny and Lise Torres."

Taro's dad took a more conventional approach, offering his hand to shake. "So you're our Taro's ghost hunter."

"Yes, sir. You're the man who didn't name him after a root vegetable." Jack snapped his mouth shut and turned a fascinating scarlet, but Taro's dad just laughed.

"True. We did not. Lautaro Maximillian Torres, for the freedom fighter and Taro's opa. If you want to really annoy him, use his full name."

"I hope you're not like those ghost hunters on TV," Mom called from the kitchen. "All that screaming and hysteria."

Jack paused in taking off his coat, peppered with late spring snow. "Um..."

"Don't be silly, Lise," Taro's dad called back.

"Those are just actors pretending to find ghosts."

When Jack leaned down to whisper in Taro's ear, his smile had finally reached his eyes. "I like your dad."

The bags revealed salad and dinner rolls and even a cheesecake from Cannelle Patisserie in Queens. The lasagna smelled heavenly, and even Taro's mom declared it still hot enough, so no further fussing was required besides setting the table. She kept casting sharp glances in Jack's direction while they ate, but beyond grilling him a bit on his family—both parents lived in Ithaca, one sister, a professor of art history at SUNY— she didn't try to make him uncomfortable as she had with Craig. She really hadn't liked Craig. Taro understood why in hindsight, but back then, her barely civil treatment of him had nearly caused a rift between them.

"So the little men from fairy tales will come tonight, you think?" Taro's dad asked as he pushed back from the table, nothing but crumbs on his cake plate.

"Think so, sir." Jack drummed his fingers on the table and immediately stopped himself. "Need to make ourselves scarce though, you and me."

"Oh?"

"They're trying to communicate with Taro. More big humans could scare them off. Um, they probably don't like me much."

Taro's dad laughed as he set his napkin on the

table. "All those cameras and recording things. They just might be a little ticked off at you. We'll go out when it gets later, then. Do you drink, Jack?"

That sounded ominous, but maybe letting Papi have some time with Jack was a good idea. He'd see how charming and smart Jack was. An ally for future defenses against Mom, if necessary. They left the condo at a little after eleven, and Taro worked on getting the little guest plate and thimbles set up for his smaller guests.

His mother was silent throughout the procedure until she took a seat on one of the stools at the kitchen island and said softly, *"Echte heinzelmännchen?"*

"Ja, Mami. Ich glaube so."

"Wie fantastisch."

At midnight, they turned the kitchen lights off, just leaving a little night light on by the toaster. When they talked, they spoke softly in German, hoping that the little people understood. Almost an hour later, little figures began to appear on the counter, hesitantly, anxiously. It was impossible to see where they came from, but suddenly they were there, creeping close to the plate with its tiny brownie portions.

The first one sat cross-legged by the plate and took a bit of brownie without glancing away from Taro and his mother. Soon a second joined and a third. Now that they were still, Taro could see they weren't little men at all. The only real resemblance to humans was a bipedal body and delicate hands and feet.

They had proportionately huge ears, with the red inner portion pointing outward, ears that towered over their heads like a jackrabbit's, the tops meeting so that the ears could have been mistaken for pointed red hats. *Maybe where the gnome legends come from? Little men in pointed red hats.*

Their eyes were obviously dark-adapted, round, again disproportionately large, which made them look like little chibis. Fine, downy fur covered their faces and possibly the rest of them, though that was hard to say, since they wore tunics and pants that might have had patterns painted on or had been heavily embroidered. Hard to see in the dim light.

Taro waited until the migration around the dish seemed to have ended, seventeen of the tiny creatures staring at him from the counter, passing thimbles of juice between them.

"Mami," Taro whispered. "Please tell them that they're welcome as long as they want to stay, but see if you can find out why they're here."

She nodded, her hands clenched on her knees the only sign that she wasn't as calm as she pretended. The first *heinzelmann* answered for the others in the high-pitched voice from Jack's recording. His mother leaned forward more and more to hear, and she spoke for some time with the head *heinzelmann*. Finally, she drew in a long breath and let it out slowly.

"They followed you because your head sings. I don't know what that means. They thought you needed them, so they went with you. But they thought you were just taking a trip and would go right back to Marburg. You kept going, and they were frightened. Then you stopped here, and the... I think they're saying the giant came. They could mean Jack, I suppose. They feel terrible about tripping him, but they were scared."

Taro nodded. That all made a bizarre kind of sense. "Could you ask them what they want now? Do they want to stay here? Do they want to go back home?"

Again, he sat still, listening to a conversation in which he understood one word out of every five or six. The head little person gestured to the kitchen. Some of the little ones began to cry, sounds so heartbroken that Taro's throat closed up and his eyes stung.

"What is it? Why are they so upset?"

His mother reached into her purse for a tissue to dab at her eyes before she answered. "They're so unhappy. They were so pleased when you came to Marburg, knowing there would be things to do again besides dust, and there would be food in the house again. They came with you because you... I think they're saying that your sound was sad. I'm not sure. That you were lonely, maybe? But they hate it here. The smells are wrong. The sounds are wrong. And the giant is trying to catch them."

"Oh. Oh, no." Taro snagged a tissue from his mother to blow his nose. "Could you tell them that Jack was just trying to find out who they were? That I was scared and thought a ghost was following me? No one is trying to catch them."

More conversation during which the leader seemed to be frowning. Maybe it was suspicion of large people, but the other little ones had quieted.

"They would like to go home, but they don't want to go back to an empty house again," Mom finally said. "Your Marburg house was safe. They could get food in the fields nearby when they had to, but they prefer an occupied house. They like that house better than the one they lived in before, where a giant would spray poisons every few weeks."

Taro cringed, as that brought to mind Jack's exterminator comment. His brain churned and whirlpooled as he tried to think things through. *This just isn't sustainable. All of this.* "Okay. I'm going to take them home. That's the most important thing right now. I'll talk to Frau Voss about making sure the house doesn't feel so empty. Lots to think about, but getting them out of here comes first."

"You're a good boy, Taro." Mom leaned in to kiss his cheek. "Even if you don't call enough."

He just shook his head and tugged his mother out of the kitchen so the little ones could do as they pleased in peace.

Taro was half-dozing with the television on when Jack and Papi stumbled back in, giggling. *That's either a good sign or a really bad one.*

"Then he climbed onto the step stool and tried to *fly* to the couch," Taro's dad was saying through tears of laughter.

Jack nearly folded double with snickers until he spotted Taro. "Um, hi."

"Please don't tell me you're telling stories about when I was little, Papi."

"OK, I won't tell you."

This set off another set of giggles, as both of the pub-crawlers struggled out of shoes and coats. Finally, Jack managed to disentangle and control himself long enough to flop onto the sofa right next to Taro. "How'd it go?"

"It was surprising. Amazing. And sad." Taro stopped his telling when Jack's head flopped onto the back of the sofa. "I think I'll save everything for the morning. Mom, Papi, I think we better say goodnight."

With his parents off to their hotel nearby, Taro bundled a sleepy, silly Jack into bed, putting to rest Jack's claim that he was always a morose and unpleasant drunk. The evening might have been one of the strangest of Taro's life, but it was also one he would cherish. He hadn't argued with his mother, and she hadn't said a single bad thing about Jack.

Jack slept late the next morning, which wasn't a shock, while Taro made quiet arrangements to return to Germany. He got out the same suitcase he'd been using for his extended around-the-world trip to be sure the *heinzelmännchen* didn't have any doubts about his intentions.

Halfway through his packing, Jack's arm flopped over the side of the bed, barely missing Taro's nose.

"Are you alive?"

"Rrrrrmmph."

"All right. At least you're undead." Taro stood up to find one bloodshot gray eye staring at him from Jack's pillow-and-blanket cave.

Jack's first attempt at speech sounded like a melding of orcish and Klingon. The second time worked slightly better. "Going somewhere?"

"Marburg. I got a flight this evening."

"Tonight?" Suddenly, Jack was upright, pale and sleep-mussed but obviously tracking. He looked so miserable, Taro was sure it couldn't all be hangover.

"Let me snag some things for you. Stay right there." Taro went to the kitchen for water, aspirin, and coffee. By the time he came back, Jack was trying unsuccessfully to get his pants on. "Hold on, there. You're about to fall and crack your head open. Sit down. Please. Tell me what's wrong."

"You're going back to Europe. I should get out of your way."

Hurt lurked in those gray eyes, something beyond a headache, and Taro realized he was being dense. "I have *two* tickets lined up. I'd love it if you wanted to come with me, but I didn't want to assume you had time."

Jack's shoulders sagged, and he accepted Taro's offerings one by one, starting with aspirin and ending with coffee. "Sorry. Didn't know—did I make an ass of myself?"

"Last night? No. You were an adorable drunk, and my dad had a great time. Let me know when you're ready to talk about important things, like why we're going to Germany."

It didn't take long for Jack to recover far enough to hear about the previous evening and to agree that yes, they had to go.

"Poor little guys. Sounds like they've had a rough time." Jack said around bites of waffle. His appetite apparently didn't suffer from hangovers. "Sorry I scared them. Bad enough they had to deal with exterminators over there. How do they all fit in your suitcase?"

"My mom asked them that, since it seems like I would've noticed when I packed and unpacked. They said that they fit in the spaces around things. Which, okay, I don't really know what that means, but it sounds like they can pop into some other place?"

"Pocket dimensions, maybe," Jack murmured. "Some use of vibrational space. No idea."

When it came time to leave, Taro did find one of the colored plastic thimbles set atop his socks in the suitcase. He took it as a signal that the *heinzelmännchen* were all aboard and ready to go. The flight was uneventful, with Taro reading and Jack, whom he had convinced to take those over-the-counter pain meds with the sleep aid in them, sound asleep.

He woke up properly on the car ride from the airport, head swiveling in true Jack style as he tried to take in everything they passed. When the Marburger Schloss came into view, the imposing castle atop the hill, Jack dug in his pockets for a camera and spent the rest of the drive happily shutterbugging away.

Jack had come along in the hopes that if he didn't try to study the *heinzelmännchen*, they would allow him to study them. He admitted that sounded a little out there even for him, but he hoped they would become more accustomed to him as a fixture rather than a threat. He bounced around the house in a manic orgy of discovery when they arrived, exploring every nook and cranny, calling out to Taro from time to time. Taro wondered if it was to help him keep track of where Jack was.

"Love the garden!" Jack yelled from the back

terrace. "So cute! There's even a pond!"

"I've been out there, you know," Taro called from the kitchen. "Could you—"

"Fish!"

Taro gave up, shaking his head, and went back to checking supplies. Frau Voss had been there, of course, and since she now had a standing shopping list for Taro's visits, a well-populated fridge greeted him. Jack bounded into the kitchen as he closed the fridge door, with every indication of bounding on to the rest of the house, so Taro snagged his sleeve.

"Could you stay in one spot for a second so I can talk to you without yelling?"

"We're having a talk?"

"Yes. About the ROEs."

Jack sat on one of the kitchen chairs so fast it nearly tipped over. Hands folded on the table, he practically vibrated with attention, and Taro had to take a breath. If he started laughing now, he'd never get through this.

"I think one of the problems I've always had with sexual partners is I didn't really... well, at first I didn't understand *me*, but that's not it now. I haven't had a good way to explain." Taro pulled a chair up next to Jack's and took both his hands in a firm grip. "Let's say for a moment that you like carrot cake."

"I *do* like carrot cake."

"Fine, that might make it easier, but this is a

hypothetical carrot cake."

"Not sure how I feel about those."

Taro put his head on the table edge for a moment. "In our scenario, Jack likes hypothetical carrot cake."

"I'm intrigued. Go on."

"Okay, great. Now pretend that I don't like carrot cake."

"How can you not like carrot cake?"

"Jack." Taro lifted one of Jack's hands to kiss his fingers. "Focus. I like it, but hypothetical Taro does not like hypothetical carrot cake."

"Got it."

Taro pulled in a huge breath, hoping Jack was teasing. If not, this wasn't going to go well at all. "So you like carrot cake and I don't, but I know that you really like it. So sometimes I'll make it for you because I like doing things that please you. Sometimes I'll try a little bite, because your enjoyment makes a difference in mine. Or I'll lick the icing off, because I like the icing but not the whole cake."

"Mmmm. Cream cheese icing..."

"Jack, *please*."

With a little grin, Jack gripped Taro's hands tighter. "I get it. I do. But you have to tell me what constitutes icing and what's cake. And how this works best for you. I can wait until you've baked. I can, um, eat cake by myself in the shower. Not a problem. If I'm supposed to, ah, get the ingredients together first, you have to tell me though."

"I'm officially dropping the extended metaphor," Taro said, trying again to choke back a laugh. "I like touch. Holding hands, snuggling, clothed, mostly naked, all wonderful. Back rubs. Kissing, as long as it's not someone trying to eat my face off. My erogenous zones aren't the usual ones."

"Gonna take a guess here—penetration is a definite deal killer?"

"Yes. Invasion of body cavities is guaranteed to make me squirm away and get some distance. Butt, mouth, ears. Does *not* work for me. Other things? I'm better at giving than receiving."

Jack's grin had vanished. He stared at their joined hands, golden eyebrows trying to meet up. "Don't laugh. Or laugh if it helps. Date nights? Does it help to schedule?"

Completely caught off guard, Taro had to try three times to answer. "I've... never tried that. Maybe it would be better to know? But the really important thing is that I won't always finish. I usually won't, and I get really stressed and unhappy if I feel like I'm *expected* to."

"Again, please don't laugh. It's the orgasm you don't like?"

Taro shook his head. "It's not that I don't like that part. It's sex with *other people* that I'm not really interested in."

Jack slid to his knees and laid his head in Taro's lap, something that might have alarmed Taro with anyone else. There was no nuzzling, no mouthing, no going for the zipper though, just head in lap. Taro found his fingers stroking through the spiky silk of Jack's hair before he could stop himself.

"I'll never expect you to eat hypothetical carrot cake. Hope you'll tell me when you want it. Also, since we're talking, morning wood is a normal biological event, not an expectation. As is morning snuggling."

"Morning snuggling is biologically driven?"

"Yes. Sometimes." Jack snickered. "You knew what I meant."

Taro took Jack's face between his hands to lift it. "Now you tell me what you need. This thing goes both ways."

Jack's gray eyes held a universe of anxiety, and he swallowed hard before answering. "Someone who'll keep the lights on. Who can... look at me."

A jagged crack zigzagged through Taro's heart. Terrified it might break, he yanked Jack into his arms. *Don't cry. Don't.* He didn't want to think about what some idiots in Jack's past had said and done to prompt that request, but Jack was a grown man. He didn't need comfort or pity. He was pleading for someone to accept him, and that didn't sound familiar at all, did it?

Taro kissed the base of Jack's jaw, then the spot just below his earlobe. "Get undressed for me."

"Here? But—"

"There's no one here but us."

Jack looked pointedly at the kitchen counter. "The little people?"

"Are nocturnal. You still have too many clothes on."

That got him moving. Jack plunked down on his butt to wrestle with his shoes, the tip of his tongue protruding from the corner of his mouth. High-tops, of course, but he managed to yank them off before they were properly untied. Socks, sweater, T-shirt—all joined the hasty retreat from his body, though he smacked an elbow on the table and a knee on the nearest chair in his scramble to get up and shed his pants and briefs.

When he'd kicked himself free, Jack straightened, every six-foot-and-then-some gangly bit of him on display. He spread his hands in front of him, his smile uncertain as he blushed. The whole procedure might have taken twenty seconds if Taro had counted. No, he wasn't some buff and bulging gym bunny or Olympic-swimmer toned, but he had a lovely architecture inherent in his whippet-lean frame, an avian grace in his long limbs that his clothes normally hid. Even his erection managed artistic in its curved, uncut splendor.

"Jack," Taro murmured. "You're beautiful."

"You don't have to—"

Taro stood, wrapped his arms around Jack's ribs, and rested his head on Jack's shoulder. "Don't want to hear it. You're beautiful. But I knew that before you took your clothes off. Arms around me, or I'll think you don't want me here."

A whimpering moan vibrated through Jack's chest as he wrapped Taro in a tight embrace. "You feel so good. Even through all the clothes."

Taro hummed in response and kissed a line up Jack's collarbone to his throat. It *did* feel good to be held again, to have his back stroked, to have bare skin under his hands. It felt even better, since Jack enjoyed it all so much. He reached between them and took hold of Jack's cock, making Jack gasp and arch, head flung back, a barely steady C-curve surrendering his most sensitive places to Taro.

He closed his fingers around the shaft and stroked slowly, free hand on Jack's hip to steady him.

"You want to sit down?"

"No... Ohgod." Jack gasped out. "Don't stop. Don't let go. Please."

"Faster?"

Jack's answer was an incoherent moan. Taro reasoned that it must have been some time since he'd been with anyone, maybe not since the betrayal of his horrid fiancé. Either that or he was one of the most responsive humans on the planet. Also possible. This was Jack, after all. He wrapped his arm farther around Jack, who was perilously close to tipping over onto his back, and increased the rhythm of his strokes.

For his part, Jack clung to Taro's shoulders, fingers digging in, his panted breaths and moans spooling out in desperate staccato measures. His hips jerked suddenly, an uneven back and forth, nearly yanking himself out of Taro's hand. Then he cried out, a long, sharp howl as he came, shooting in high, white arcs all over the tiled kitchen floor.

Taro suddenly had most of Jack's weight in his arms, and he hooked a chair over to ease his wobbly-legged lover down. "All right there?"

He got a wheeze and a chuckle in response before Jack nuzzled his chest. "All right, he says. I'm flying. Dizzy circle flying." He wrapped his arms around Taro's waist with a happy sigh. "You make amazing carrot cake."

"Thank you. I do like making it for the right person." Taro leaned over to kiss the top of that mussed blond head, the ball of light that had lodged under his heart in Chiang Mai expanding to fill his body. Sweet, sticky, wonderful light. "Did you still want to go see the castle?"

Jack peered up with one eye from where he was still nuzzling Taro's shirt. "Short nap first?"

"Deal. Nap. Snack. Castle. In that order. I'll

clean up. You go rest. Our room's upstairs. It's the last door on the left."

He laughed softly as he listened to Jack stumble up the steps. There had been a time when cleaning up someone else's spunk would've left him gagging. He was more practical about those things now, and he didn't mind doing it this time. No resentment. No anger. He was still smiling when he went upstairs to find Jack asleep in his customary nest, head tucked under the pillows.

* * * * *

Taro woke later that night to an empty bed. He froze, trying to banish the nasty thoughts whispering at him. He used to wake up to an empty bed frequently, more toward the end of his relationship with Craig, when he was justifying his sneaking out for sex by saying that Taro was frigid and didn't even try.

No. Stop it. Stop making the comparisons. Craig's long gone. Jack probably got hungry.

Jet lag, kitchen sex, a trip to Marburg Schloss with lots of walking all probably meant that they should have had more dinner than the light bar fare they'd snagged on the way back to the house. They'd talked about what happened next, to Jack's house, since Taro wanted him to move in, and to the rest of the properties, since Taro knew his schedule wasn't sustainable. He would probably keep them and visit the ones he liked best more often while renting out the others when he wasn't there. What he wanted more than anything was to buy Jack whatever he needed, to support him in his business, but their talks had stalled on that point. They had a lot to work out, but they had time.

Taro got up and pulled on his robe, padding down the hall with a yawn. Yes, Jack's shoes were still by the door; his wool coat still hung on its peg. From these signs, Taro expected to hear the fridge opening, possibly the rattle of dishes or silverware.

He did hear something but couldn't identify it. A soft, rhythmic beat came from the kitchen, like rain pattering on the roof, though the night was clear. When he reached the kitchen, Jack stood by the entrance, peeking around the doorframe, with his hand covering his mouth in an attitude of wonder.

Taro stole up behind him and wrapped his arms around Jack's waist. "What's happening?"

"Look," Jack whispered as he pointed to the counter.

Around the plate of crumbs they now left out instead of cleaning everything up, the *heinzelmännchen* had gathered in a circle. Each of them had two pieces of metal that gleamed in the moonlight as they struck them together. *Safety pins?* Those made the *tip-tip-tip* sound, augmented by the stamping of thirty-four tiny feet.

Jack pulled him into a warm embrace, his eyes wide with helpless wonder. "Taro, they're *dancing.*"

"They are. I think they're happy now." Taro nestled against him, watching the stomping, clicking, and occasional leaping as the *heinzelmännchen* turned and spun about each other. The warm glow inside Taro felt like it was trying to expand and encompass the house, the town, the world. "I think I know how they feel."

* * * * *

"Uncle Taro!"

Ah, nothing like the put-upon summons of a seven-year-old to make you forget what you're thinking. Taro looked up from his tablet as the mini-herd of nieces and nephews stampeded toward him. Of course, this was the under-nine contingent. The over-the-age-of-twelve batch would never condescend to trample or gallop, much less stampede. By the tone, Taro was almost certain this would be a complaint against one of the many unfair adults in the house.

"Yes, Jenna?"

"Daddy says we can't go to the beach tomorrow without adult supervision, but *he's* taking Kayla and Matty and them *kayaking.*"

Taro fought a smile so hard his face hurt. Luka's betrayal of choosing the hated and revered older kids over the younger ones was obviously unforgivable.

"Yes. I heard about that," Taro said and put his feet back up on his lawn chaise.

"Uncle T*aro*!"

"Hmm?" He pretended to read his screen. "Was there something you wanted to ask me?"

"Would you *pleeeease* take us?"

Taro looked up at the wide blue Prince Edward Island sky, unimpeded here by any man-made structure. A deeper blue was just seeping in from the east, evening finally catching up to the long summer day at this latitude. "Right now?"

"No, silly." Jenna rolled her eyes in a good imitation of her older sister. "You can't go to the beach at night."

"Oh, I see. Is tomorrow soon enough?"

"Yes. Please."

"All right. Mr. Jack and I will take you tomorrow."

The herd gave a collective shout of joy and stampeded back toward the house, presumably to torment some other grown-up. Jack sidestepped them as he sauntered down the outside steps and dropped down onto the grass beside Taro's chair.

"Volunteering me?"

Taro stretched out an arm to let Jack lean over to rest his head on Taro's chest. "I'll unvolunteer you if you want. But you did want to see the beach and the lighthouse."

"Still do. Kidding. I'll go."

The kids, regardless of age, had taken a liking to Jack. The parents didn't want them calling him *Jack* though, and he wasn't comfortable with *Uncle Jack*, so he'd agreed to *Mr. Jack*, though he thought it was hilarious.

Jack tipped his head back. "Sky's so clear here. Makes me dizzy sometimes."

"Are you enjoying yourself though? If you don't stare at the sky too hard?"

"I am." Jack wrapped an arm around Taro's waist with a contented sigh. "Wouldn't want to *live* out here. But it's nice. Quiet. Little guys doing okay?"

"I'm pretty sure they are, but I'll check in with them tonight."

After much discussion, much of it involving pastries, they'd come to a compromise. Jack would accompany Taro on his trips as long as he didn't have a case, and Taro would give up his strict schedules and allow for where they *wanted* to go instead of where he thought he had to go. Through the spring, they'd explored Barcelona and Paris, and as summer approached, they'd broached the idea with the family of a get-together on the island. While work didn't allow most of the adults to take more than a two-week vacation, two weeks was more than they'd been able to have as a family for years. Everyone had jumped at the chance.

The old white farmhouse didn't have bedrooms to accommodate everyone, so Ray had brought a couple of big tents for the older kids, while the little ones bedded down with sleeping bags in their parents' rooms. Chaotic, messy, loud, the arrangement did tug at Taro's nerves at the end of each day, but this was family. He wanted to be here with them, and they accepted Jack without question. Eventually, the comparisons with Craig even died away as they got to know him.

As far as the *heinzelmännchen* were concerned, Taro (with Frau Voss's help) had given them a choice. They could stay in the Marburg house as long as they liked and never be disturbed, or they could travel with him sometimes, to places they wanted to go. The little ones put their heads together in a flurry of whispered conversation, and when they finally reached a consensus, they had decided they liked the house in Wales and the one on PEI, and that they would like to discuss others with him.

As for New York? They never wanted to go back.

8Taro kissed Jack's forehead and stroked the spikes of golden hair turning silver in the soft light of evening. Yes, he was writing, but it was no longer a frantic catalogue of things seen and food eaten. His travelogues had become quieter, warmer things about how places felt and about encounters with the people in them. This was better. So much better.

"Should let them choose," Jack said in a sleepy murmur.

"I thought so too. We have a system worked out." Taro gave him a little squeeze. "You want to help me set it up, or should I put you to bed?"

"Hmm. Just nice here. Listening." Jack nuzzled at Taro's shirt. "Crickets. Your heart." With a twitch, Jack sat up. "What system?"

"Ah, I figured that might wake you up." Taro chuckled and leaned in for a soft kiss, though Jack was obviously focused on *heinzelmännchen* updates. "Come on. I'll show you."

Jack unfolded from the grass and helped Taro out of the lawn chaise, which seemed determined to eat him. When they reached the kitchen, Taro pulled a manila folder out of the drawer under the new toaster. The old one hadn't been as hardy as the ancient refrigerator and had tried to start a kitchen fire in its last throes. He opened the folder and took out printouts of photos on the counter, lining them up in a neat, precisely even row.

"Ah. I've been there." Jack's grin could've lit up the coast as he pointed to the picture of the Chiang Mai property. "What's the signal?"

"The *heinzelmännchen* will put all the photos away except the one they want. I have the feeling they'll pick Chiang Mai next. They were eyeing it when I showed them how to pick a destination. But they wanted privacy to decide."

"That'd be rough, going back, but I'll manage." Jack wrapped his arms around Taro, his bright eyes twinkling.

"You never did have that naked swim."

"Could bring a suit."

Taro tapped a hand on his sternum. "I'd rather you didn't."

"Voyeur."

"Only sometimes." *Mostly since you.* "I like watching you."

Jack's smile softened to something warm and tender. He pulled Taro close and drew in a shuddering breath. "Anyone else, that would've been sarcasm."

"Anyone else would be an idiot, then." Taro reached up to take Jack's face between his hands.

The kiss had a hint of heat in it, but no pressure, especially since a moment later, Jack was staring at the photos, eyebrows drawn together, gaze distant and unfocused.

"Jack? What's going on in that brain?"

"Just wondering," he murmured. "Might be able... Think they'd let me take spectroscopy readings? When they go into their pocket dimensions?"

Taro saw conference calls with Frau Voss in his future and a certain someone enthusing over new pieces of equipment. All part of his new world. He wouldn't have had it any other way.

THE END

Dear Reader

Thank you for purchasing **Uncommonly Tidy Poltergeists**. If Angel had you laughing with the *Brimstone* boys, you should check out her *Offbeat Crimes* series—who doesn't love a paranormal misfits squad? Or if you prefer a little sci fi action, how about a drag queen AI—in Space? Angel's *Brimstone* crew will keep you laughing and on the edge of your seat with their adventures in space.

Please consider leaving a review where you purchased this ebook or on Goodreads. Reviews and word-of-mouth recommendations are vital to independent publishers.

We love hearing from our readers. You can email us at mischiefcornerbooks@gmail.com. To read excerpts from all our titles, visit our website: http://www.mischiefcornerbooks.com.

Sincerely,
Mischief Corner Books

Potato Surprise

A Brimstone Prequel

Angel Martinez

http://www.mischiefcornerbooks.com

Brandywine
Investigations

OPEN for Business

Angel Martinez

http://www.mischiefcornerbooks.com

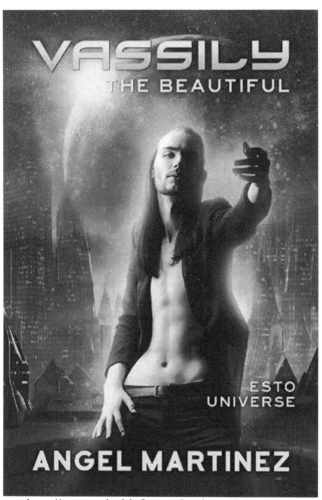

http://www.mischiefcornerbooks.com

About Angel Martinez

While Angel Martinez is the erotic fiction pen name of a writer of several genres, she writes both kinds of gay romance – Science Fiction and Fantasy. Currently living part time in the hectic sprawl of northern Delaware, (and full time inside the author's head) Angel has one husband, one son, two cats, a changing variety of other furred and scaled companions, a love of all things beautiful and a terrible addiction to the consumption of both knowledge and chocolate.

For more information on Angel's work, please visit:

Official Website:
Erotic Fiction for the Hungry Mind

Facebook:
https://www.facebook.com/Angel.Martinez.author

Goodreads:
http://www.goodreads.com/author/show/
1010469.Angel_Martinez

Email:
angelmartinezauthor@gmail.com

Also by Angel Martinez

BRANDYWINE INVESTIGATIONS
Brandywine Investigations: Open for Business (Omnibus)

BRIMSTONE
Potato Surprise: A Brimstone Prequel
Hell for the Company #1
Fear of Frogs #2
Shax's War #3
Beside a Black Tarn #4
Brimstone: Demon Owned & Operated (Omnibus #1 - 3)
The Brimstone Journals: Collection One

THE ENDANGERED FAE SERIES
Finn
Diego
Semper Fae
No Fae is an Island

ESTO UNIVERSE
Vassily the Beautiful
Prisoner 374215
Gravitational Attraction

INTERPLANETARY MULTISPECIES PACT (IMP)
A Christmas Cactus for the General
A Message from the Home Office*

*Part of the *Foolish Encounters* Anthology

OFFBEAT CRIMES
Lime Gelatin and Other Monsters
Pill Bugs of Time

VARIANT CONFIGURATIONS
Rarely Pure & Never Simple

SINGLE TITLES
The Color of His Crest
Hearts & Flowers: A Tale of Hay Fever and Bad Decor
Restoration
The Line
Meteor Strike: Serge and Een

AURA UNIVERSE (with Bellora Quinn)
Quinn's Gambit
Flax's Pursuit
Kellen's Awakening

About Mischief Corner Books

Mischief Corner Books is an organization of superheroes… no, it's a platinum-album techno-fusion group… no, hold on a sec here…

Ah yes. Mischief Corner Books is a diverse group of authors who met on a mountain in Tennessee and decided since they were probably too easily distracted to rule the world that they'd settle for causing a bit of mayhem instead.

In addition to making mayhem, we publish books with a diverse range of genres and topics... we live to break molds.

MCB. Giving voice to LGBTQ fiction.

Website:
http://www.mischiefcornerbooks.com

Made in the USA
Lexington, KY
25 October 2019

55975857R00101